THE PRACTICE OF PRYING

THE SIDEKICK'S SURVIVAL GUIDE MYSTERIES, BOOK 4

CHRISTY BARRITT

COMPLETE BOOK LIST

Squeaky Clean Mysteries:

#1 Hazardous Duty

#2 Suspicious Minds

#2.5 It Came Upon a Midnight Crime (novella)

#3 Organized Grime

#4 Dirty Deeds

#5 The Scum of All Fears

#6 To Love, Honor and Perish

#7 Mucky Streak

#8 Foul Play

#9 Broom & Gloom

#10 Dust and Obey

#11 Thrill Squeaker

#11.5 Swept Away (novella)

#12 Cunning Attractions

#13 Cold Case: Clean Getaway

#14 Cold Case: Clean Sweep

#15 Cold Case: Clean Break

#16 Cleans to an End (coming soon)

While You Were Sweeping, A Riley Thomas Spinoff

The Sierra Files:

#1 Pounced

#2 Hunted

#3 Pranced

#4 Rattled

The Gabby St. Claire Diaries (a Tween Mystery series):

The Curtain Call Caper

The Disappearing Dog Dilemma

The Bungled Bike Burglaries

The Worst Detective Ever

#1 Ready to Fumble

#2 Reign of Error

#3 Safety in Blunders

#4 Join the Flub

#5 Blooper Freak

#6 Flaw Abiding Citizen

#7 Gaffe Out Loud

#8 Joke and Dagger

#9 Wreck the Halls

#10 Glitch and Famous (coming soon)

Raven Remington
Relentless 1
Relentless 2 (coming soon)

Holly Anna Paladin Mysteries:
#1 Random Acts of Murder
#2 Random Acts of Deceit
#2.5 Random Acts of Scrooge
#3 Random Acts of Malice
#4 Random Acts of Greed
#5 Random Acts of Fraud
#6 Random Acts of Outrage
#7 Random Acts of Iniquity

Lantern Beach Mysteries
#1 Hidden Currents
#2 Flood Watch
#3 Storm Surge
#4 Dangerous Waters
#5 Perilous Riptide
#6 Deadly Undertow

Lantern Beach Romantic Suspense
Tides of Deception
Shadow of Intrigue

The Art of Eavesdropping

The Perks of Meddling

The Exercise of Interfering

The Practice of Prying (coming soon)

Carolina Moon Series

Home Before Dark

Gone By Dark

Wait Until Dark

Light the Dark

Taken By Dark

Suburban Sleuth Mysteries:

Death of the Couch Potato's Wife

Fog Lake Suspense:

Edge of Peril

Margin of Error

Brink of Danger

Line of Duty

Cape Thomas Series:

Dubiosity

Disillusioned

Distorted

Standalone Romantic Mystery:

The Good Girl

Suspense:
Imperfect
The Wrecking

Sweet Christmas Novella:
Home to Chestnut Grove

Standalone Romantic-Suspense:
Keeping Guard
The Last Target
Race Against Time
Ricochet
Key Witness
Lifeline
High-Stakes Holiday Reunion
Desperate Measures
Hidden Agenda
Mountain Hideaway
Dark Harbor
Shadow of Suspicion
The Baby Assignment
The Cradle Conspiracy
Trained to Defend

Nonfiction:

Characters in the Kitchen

Changed: True Stories of Finding God through Christian Music (out of print)

The Novel in Me: The Beginner's Guide to Writing and Publishing a Novel (out of print)

CHAPTER ONE

"DID YOU HEAR?"

As soon as I walked into the Driscoll and Associates office, Velma Wells, our administrative assistant, stood from her desk near the front door and hurried toward me.

I stopped in my tracks when I heard the ominous tone in her voice. Had something happened to my boss, Oscar, over the weekend? Or maybe to my coworker, Michael?

Concern pulsed through me. "No, what's going on?"

"The Beltway Killer struck again." Velma's voice sounded low and gravelly as she leaned toward me, the curly blonde hair piled up high on her head falling into her eyes. "The victim's body was found this morning about three miles from Storm River."

The breath left my lungs. I didn't know much about the infamous serial killer, but I knew enough. The monster had been hunting women in this area for the past three years, and four victims had been found so far. His name came from the fact that he always targeted areas near the Capital Beltway around Washington, DC.

Residents had been struck with terror ever since the killings began. Citizens double-checked their locks every night. People, especially single women, didn't go out by themselves after dark. A general sense of tension and foreboding filled the air.

"That's terrible." I gripped the travel coffee mug I'd brought from home. "Do you know anything else?"

"Only what I heard on the news." Velma's hand went to her slender hip as her eyes widened. "The victim was in her early twenties and was from Storm River. I'm so upset."

As she should be. The tragic loss of life should always be mourned.

"Thanks for letting me know," I said. "Does this have anything to do with our next case?"

Velma's animated face changed from sad to flabbergasted. "This? No. Of course not. Oscar is waiting for you in his office."

Of course he was. I hadn't really thought anything would change, and maybe it shouldn't.

I worked for a private investigator. Actually, I hesitated to even call him a private investigator most of the time. Oscar Driscoll was simply the man who sat in an office, called the shots, and paid the bills. Meanwhile, my coworker, Michael Straley, and I were the ones who did all the footwork.

Oscar was fine with that as long as he got all of the credit and glory.

On the other hand, Michael had been a great teacher to me, showing me the ropes of investigating. But I still had a lot to learn.

With a touch of hesitation, I stepped toward Oscar's office. When I walked in, I saw Oscar and Michael chatting like old friends. But the conversation stopped as soon as they saw me.

I wasn't sure how Michael had wormed his way into Oscar's good graces so easily. Me, on the other hand? I'd only worked here a month, and I'd already been fired twice and threatened with more. I fully expected to be fired again before too long. The question was: Would Oscar take me back next time or not?

Oscar had been a police detective before he'd left the force for some unknown reason—unknown to me, at least. He was in his fifties and on the larger side, with a thick light brown mustache and an overall lazy work ethic.

Michael, conversely, was almost thirty. He had a squarish face, framed by a shadowy beard and mustache, and a thick muscular build. He liked to wear his baseball caps backward, paired with quirky T-shirts and loafers.

"Elliot!" Oscar's voice sounded perkier than usual. "Have a seat."

I glanced at Michael, feeling a tad suspicious. Despite that, I lowered myself into the seat beside Michael and waited to hear what my task would be for the day.

"What do you know about softball, Elliot?" Oscar asked.

My eyebrows shot up. "Softball?"

Was I supposed to know something about it?

I wasn't exactly a sporty kind of girl. No, give me a book and a cup of tea any day, and I'd be content.

"That's right," Oscar said. "Every year, Storm River hosts a big softball game that pits local business leaders against local politicians. It's called the Bigwigs vs. the Baby Kissers."

"Bigwigs? Baby kissers?" What in the world was he talking about?

"Bosses are sometimes called bigwigs because men of importance in times past used to wear wigs," Michael explained. "And politicians used to be known as baby kissers because it was a campaigning technique."

I suppose that made sense. But I still wasn't sure what this had to do with me or with investigating anything.

"Practices have been well underway," Oscar continued. "The game is this Saturday, after all, so there's only a week of practice left. All the money raised at the game goes to a local food bank. People in this town take the competition very seriously."

Apparently, people in this town took any type of contest seriously. Just last week, I'd participated in a lip-synching competition, and I was surprised at how people were fully invested—and determined—to win.

"So what's the problem?" I finally asked, tired of dancing around the fire as if I didn't have a guinea pig to roast. That was a Yerbian expression.

"The coach for the Bigwigs, a man named James Cruz, mysteriously died over the weekend," Oscar said. "On the outside, his death may not look suspicious—he was in a car crash—but some people are convinced that it was no accident. We've been hired to investigate."

"Okay . . ." I felt like there was something I was missing here.

"Michael is going to take over as the coach for the team, and you, Dora—"

"Don't call me that," I warned. Just because I liked the jungle didn't mean I liked to be compared to a cartoon character.

"You, *Elliot*, are going to be his girlfriend."

My eyebrows wedged together as those words sank in. "I don't understand. Why would that help solve this case?"

"Michael is a shoo-in as the team coach," Oscar said.

"True fact," Michael said.

I understood that part. Michael had played professional baseball, so it made sense. It was the girlfriend part and the fact that we had to go undercover that confused me.

"The person who hired us, game coordinator Wally Winders, firmly believes somebody on the team is responsible for Cruz's death." Oscar stared at me, as if waiting for my thoughts to catch up.

"Go on," I said.

"Cruz was forty-two and divorced," Oscar said. "He was a former high school baseball coach who, just four years ago, began working as a consultant for a national chain of gyms. He's led the Bigwigs to victory the past three years."

"Why does this Wally guy think he was murdered?" I asked.

"Some weird things have been happening lately. Random acts of vandalism. Cruz wasn't acting like himself. Plus, the car accident raised some red flags."

"How does someone murder someone else via a car accident?" I had to ask the question. I couldn't wrap my mind around that idea.

"Maybe the brake line was cut," Michael suggested. "I have a copy of the accident report. I'm going to take it to my friend later so he can look at it. Another possibility is that someone ran him off the road and then drove off. There were no skid marks, which seems suspicious."

"Drugs or alcohol in his system?" I asked.

"Tox screen says no," Michael said.

"Why would someone on the team be responsible?" I asked, still trying to figure out what exactly we were going to be investigating.

"The vandalisms seem to be centered on the team," Oscar said. "Plus, Coach Cruz died after leaving practice. We're being paid to find out if his death was malicious or not. I need you two to get to the heart of the matter."

"Why do I have to pretend to be Michael's girlfriend?" Yeah, I was still stuck on that.

"Because nobody is going to believe that you are qualified to be an assistant coach," Oscar said with a snort. "I haven't even seen you play, and I know that."

I might have been offended if his words weren't true. "But if people around town are participating, aren't they going to know Michael and I aren't actually dating?"

"As much as the two of you are seen together, I don't really think that's going to be a problem." Oscar shrugged, as if it was a foregone conclusion.

I felt my cheeks heat for a moment.

I couldn't argue with that either. Michael and I *had* been hanging out a lot. Not only on the job, but we'd done some activities outside of work. I'd also been spending time with his daughter, Chloe, including going to a Muffins with Mom event recently.

Maybe the idea wouldn't be so much of a stretch—to anyone looking in from the outside, at least.

"I'll do whatever I need to," I finally said.

"Good. I was hoping you were going to say that. Now, here's everything you need to know to get started." Oscar handed me a file before glancing at his watch. "The team's next practice is tonight. Michael will have to show you the rest."

I glanced at Michael, who held a vague amusement in his eyes. He had no idea what he was getting into, did he? Because my first instinct when I saw a ball coming at me was to duck.

"Okay," I said. "Let's go score a touchdown."

Michael groaned. "A home run, Elliot. Touchdowns are for football."

"Of course. Let's go get a home run."

I had a lot to learn about this game. Like *a lot* a lot.

A FEW HOURS LATER, Michael and I finished reviewing the basics of the case.

When we were done, Oscar told us to take a few hours for ourselves since Michael and I would be on the clock this evening. It worked out perfectly because I'd told Police Detective Dylan Hunter I'd meet him for lunch.

Given everything that had happened with the Beltway Killer, I double-checked to make sure he could still meet. He told me he could.

A few minutes later, I pulled up to my favorite restaurant, a place called The Boardroom. It featured charcuterie boards and board games, which was the perfect combination, if you asked me.

Hunter was already there when I walked in. I supposed I could call him by his first name, but he'd simply become

"Hunter" to me. A smile stretched across my face when I saw him. The man was handsome. Lean and trim, with classic good looks and a reserved manner.

There was something about him that reminded me of Captain America. I didn't watch much TV, but my sister, Ruth, had forced me to watch that movie, and I'd quickly learned who Chris Evans was. I gave him two thumbs up—and the same for Hunter.

He stood and gave me a quick hug before we sat across from each other.

We weren't exactly dating. Instead, we were getting to know each other.

Both of us had dramatic—or should I say traumatic?—romantic histories. Hunter's included his fiancée being killed at the hands of the Beltway Killer.

Mine included being ghosted by my fiancé before I fled a country halfway across the world.

His was far worse. And I knew that today was going to be a difficult day for him, which was another reason I was glad he was still meeting with me.

"I already ordered a pretzel board for us," he said. "I hope that's okay. It sounded like the perfect comfort food for today."

I reached across the table and squeezed his hand. I tried to put myself in his shoes. I could only imagine how he felt. "How are you?"

A shadow fell over his gaze, and tension stretched across his face. "I don't know, to be honest."

"I imagine that every time you hear about a new victim it has to be difficult." I didn't know if he wanted to talk about this or not, but I didn't want to miss the opportunity in case he needed to.

"It is."

My throat tightened at the confirmation. The reality of the situation was absolutely terrifying. "Are you working the case?"

He rubbed his jaw, as if trying to hide how hard this was on him. "No, the chief won't let me. Says I'm too close to it. Logically, I know he's correct. But emotionally . . . I really want to jump in. It's probably a good thing that you and I are meeting for lunch today. Otherwise, I might find myself right in the middle of things when I'm not supposed to be."

I could relate. I did that a lot. "Is it true the victim was from Storm River?"

He shrugged. "I can't tell you. Not yet. But as soon as that information is able to be shared, the media will announce it."

"Of course." I hadn't expected him to be able to give me details. I was probably asking too many questions anyway.

As his phone rang, he stood and paced away from the table. I could hear only part of the conversation, but what I did pick up on had me curious.

He muttered something about a rose and a nautical knot.

What did that mean? I knew I couldn't ask. I'd already posed too many questions.

"Thanks for the update," Hunter said before putting his phone away and coming to sit across from me again. He smiled, as if the conversation hadn't been a big deal.

But I couldn't help but wonder what he'd been talking about, and if it had something to do with the Beltway Killer.

CHAPTER TWO

"SORRY ABOUT THAT," Hunter said, just as our pretzel board was delivered.

I picked up a hot dog wrapped in a pretzel and dipped it into some cheese sauce. "No problem."

"Enough about me and my work. How is everything with you? How's your sister?"

I frowned at the mention of Ruth. "Her coughing fits have been getting worse just over the past few days. She did move up on the transplant list, but it's always a little frightening to see her going downhill so fast like this. She doesn't want to admit it, but I know she's struggling right now."

Ruth had cystic fibrosis, a lung disease. The condition was life-threatening, as the body produced a sticky, thick mucus that coated her lungs.

"As anyone would be in her shoes." Empathy filled Hunter's gaze. "Your mom holding on okay?"

I shrugged. "She's my mom. She worries about everything. Especially my sister and me. But sometimes, when you're going through something like this, the best thing you can do is to keep marching forward."

Hunter's eyes met mine, and I knew he understood. He'd been through hard times too. Those times, if we let them, allowed us to grow stronger and deepened our character.

"It's true." He shifted. "How about work? You staying busy?"

My stomach twisted into a knot. This was where things got tricky. Since Hunter was a detective and I was an apprentice for a local PI, I never knew exactly what I could tell him. I didn't want to cross any boundaries or say anything I wasn't supposed to.

It might get me fired. Then again, what was new?

But I wasn't sure what harm it could do to share a little bit about this case. Maybe it would help keep Hunter's mind off of the Beltway Killer for a few minutes.

"Michael and I are working with the Bigwigs vs. the Baby Kissers," I said.

"What's so mysterious about that show of arrogance?"

I smiled. Hunter shared my viewpoint on some of the attitudes of people here in town. Most of the people were not only wealthy, but they thought highly of themselves. Too highly.

"Wally Winders thinks that the coach was murdered."

One of his eyebrows rose. "James Cruz died in a car accident. It was a tragedy, yes. But the investigation was open and closed. The road was slick, he texted someone, and he hit a tree. There were no signs of foul play."

He'd texted someone? Why hadn't that come up in my earlier conversation with Oscar? Interesting.

And it made it seem like more of an accident, for sure.

I shrugged, trying to play it off like I'd known that fact. "I know the authorities say it was an accident. But some people think he was intentionally killed."

"Why in the world would someone think that he was murdered?" Hunter sounded truly stumped.

"I guess some mysterious incidents happened before he died. Michael and I are meeting with someone tomorrow to hear exactly what they were."

Hunter looked unconvinced as he lifted a shoulder in a shrug. "I hope you'll be able to find some of the answers you're looking for."

"Me too."

For the rest of lunch, Hunter and I kept our conversation simple. It had been fun talking and getting to know the man a little better. He was on the quiet side, someone who liked to think before he spoke, and he had a great smile.

But now it was time for Michael and me to meet. We had a lot to talk about.

Like *a lot* a lot.

Not only had the Beltway Killer struck again and had this coach possibly died by homicide. Michael and I also had another case on the side: the possible murder of my father.

I MET Michael back at the office, and we hopped into his minivan. We were going to pay a visit to his friend Grayson, who lived closer to the DC area.

A rumble of nerves rushed through me as I thought about the quickly approaching meeting. Michael had gone to college with Grayson Whittier, a man who now worked as a computer expert for the CIA. He was helping us overcome an . . . obstacle, for lack of a better word . . . we'd encountered in our quest to find answers about my father's death.

"You sure you're ready for this?" Michael glanced at me with concern.

I stared out the window at the city streets as they blurred past. "As ready as I will ever be, I guess. Grayson didn't tell you what he found?"

"No, he didn't say what it was. Just that he needed to talk to us in person."

Michael and I had dropped off a jump drive I'd found in my father's possessions. I didn't know what was on the device, but I had a feeling the contents were worth killing over, and that was precisely why a man affiliated with my father had recently been murdered.

My life was a twisted, winding mess right now. To summarize it all, my family and I had moved here from the South American country of Yerba about four months ago. Only a month after we moved, my father had died from a heart attack. About four weeks ago, I had discovered a secret journal he'd kept, where I'd learned he'd been a spy for our home country. The journal also indicated that his death may not have been natural or accidental.

That fact had confirmed to me that the people I'd sensed were watching me were, indeed, actually watching me. But then, just last week, someone who'd been a colleague of my father had been murdered while trying to get in touch with me. It turned out there were multiple people here in the US who were operatives for the new regime that had taken over in Yerba. They'd had a special focus on my father. Now that he was dead, they apparently had a special focus on me.

Confusing, right? I could hardly keep it all straight myself.

That was why Michael's IT friend was trying to help us decrypt the jump drive. He'd apparently found something intriguing on it and wanted to talk to us face-to-face.

Excitement, curiosity, and a bit of fear washed through me. I had no idea what Grayson might tell us.

"So how was your date with Hunter?" Michael asked as we cruised along the interstate.

"It wasn't really a date," I said. "Like I said before, we're just getting to know each other. No pressure."

"So how was your *noncommittal* date? Did he apologize again for kissing you?"

I shot him a dirty look. "I'm going to pretend you didn't say that. It was good. We had good conversation and good food. I can't complain."

"Did he tell you anything about this Beltway Killer?"

"He said he couldn't. I'll have to learn the details from the media reports."

"All of this getting to know each other, and he can't even pull any strings for you?" Michael shook his head in mock disappointment.

I jolted my arm out and punched his tattooed bicep. "You don't really think I would try that, do you?"

Michael glanced at me and smiled. "No, I don't. You nearly have an anxiety attack every time we have to make up a cover story."

We pulled into the parking garage of Grayson's apartment complex. The place was on the swankier side, but not so expensive that it was gated. Still, all the finishings were high-end and modern.

We took the stairs to the second floor, where Grayson's place was located.

But as we reached his door, I noticed it wasn't latched.

Michael pushed his arm back, stopping me from going any farther. His lightheartedness turned into concern faster than a trap-jaw ant springing on a victim. "You should stay here."

Apprehension ricocheted through me.

All the scenarios rushing through my mind weren't just paranoia. Michael was obviously concerned also.

I lingered near the doorway as Michael pushed the door open. As he did, I caught a glance of what was inside.

Chaos.

Someone had been here. Furnishings were turned over. Shelves emptied. Pictures smashed.

I squeezed my eyes shut for a moment, trying to prepare myself for the implications of what had happened.

There was only one thing I knew to do. Rhyme.

It's what I always did when I needed to keep my thoughts occupied.

Why can't things just be easy? Today's events are making me queasy. Something is majorly wrong. My quest for answers is taking too long. Too many have already been hurt. That fact makes me feel like dirt.

I wished the dirt part was just because I couldn't think of another rhyming word.

But it wasn't.

If Grayson had been injured—or worse—it was all my fault.

CHAPTER THREE

MICHAEL EMERGED a few minutes later with a grim look on his face. "Grayson's not here."

My alarm continued to grow until my head pounded. "You just talked to him, right?"

Michael nodded stiffly and reached for his phone. "I did about an hour ago. He told me he would be here. But clearly somebody else got to him first."

Nausea rose in me. I'd never meant for any of this to happen. I should have known better than to get anyone else involved.

Michael dialed something on his phone and waited. A moment later, he lowered it and shook his head, his jaw tightening. "Grayson's not answering his phone."

"Someone grabbed him, didn't they?" I hardly wanted to speak the words aloud.

"It's my best guess. I have to call the police."

I didn't argue with him. If his friend's life was in danger, we clearly needed to let the proper authorities know.

But if this had happened because of that jump drive and essentially because of me then I wouldn't be able to forgive myself. I had never intended to put this man in danger when I asked him to help.

After Michael dialed 911 and they told us the police were on their way, he put his phone away. "I figure we have about five minutes to look through everything here and see if we can find out anything about Grayson's disappearance before the cops arrive. We need to look for any evidence about who took him, what happened, or where he might be."

I nodded, grateful that Michael wasn't going to be a stickler here. No doubt if someone had grabbed Grayson, they had grabbed that jump drive too. But had Grayson left any other evidence? Had he printed anything that had been on the jump drive?

I had no idea, but I needed to know for myself if it was a possibility.

I followed Michael into the apartment.

The inside looked worse than I'd thought it would. Everything had been torn up, and it almost looked like there had been a fight. Furniture was overturned, pictures were off the walls, and books were on the floor.

How had none of the neighbors heard anything? Things had to have been loud and jarring to get to this point.

I stepped over some broken pictures, passed some smashed plates, and nearly tripped over a gutted house plant.

We went straight into Grayson's office. The place had been set up almost like a cave, with six monitors on the desk and the windows blacked out. Papers were strewn everywhere, file drawers stood open, and one of the monitors had been smashed.

I had no idea exactly what had happened to Grayson, but it hadn't been good.

Dear Lord . . . be with him.

I glanced at the floor and saw a small trail of blood there. "Look, Michael."

As he glanced down, his jaw tightened even more. "Yes, I know. I saw that."

My fears were confirmed. Grayson had been hurt.

Quickly, I looked through the contents on the desk, in the drawers, and on the floor.

My jump drive was gone, and I didn't see any evidence of what could have been on it.

I had thought we were so close to finding some answers. To figuring out the secret my father knew that had put his life in danger. The secret that was now putting my life—and the lives of my mom and sister—in danger.

Michael stepped into the living room and glanced out the window. "The police are here. We better get out."

Quickly, we left the apartment and stepped into the hallway.

As we did, two officers emerged from the elevator.

"Do we tell them about the jump drive?" I whispered.

Michael's gaze clouded. "Do we want to open that up for other people to know? The more people who know, the trickier this becomes."

"But Grayson works for the CIA. If I withhold this information and it hinders finding Grayson . . ." The choice pulled so fiercely within me that my stomach ached.

He glanced at the officers. "I don't think it's a good idea. But it's your information, your call."

I had to figure that out, and I had to figure it out quickly.

MICHAEL and I were instructed to wait out in the hallway while the police officers examined the space. As we stood there, the door next to Grayson's place popped open. A short man in his thirties with red hair stuck his head out. He didn't bother to hide his curiosity.

"Everything okay out here?" A slight lisp captured his words.

I glanced at Michael, deciding to let him take the lead here. My head was still pounding with equal parts guilt and anxiety.

"Appears somebody broke into your neighbor's place," Michael said. "Did you hear anything?"

"I heard some banging around, but I was wearing my AirPods. It helps when I listen to white noise as I work. But I felt the walls rattle and wondered if something was up."

"Did you come over to check it out?" Michael asked.

"As soon as I heard the noise, it stopped. I figured maybe Grayson was working out or had dropped something. When I didn't hear anything else, I let it go." The man frowned. "I guess that was a bad idea."

"The police are probably going to want to talk to you," Michael said.

His forehead wrinkled. "Is everything okay? Did something happen to Grayson?"

Michael and I exchanged glances.

"He's not there," Michael said.

The neighbor's eyes widened. "That doesn't sound good. I guess I should have been more vigilant. The complex is usually so safe . . ."

"Listen, if you hear anything, let us know." Michael handed him a card.

The man took it, read the words there, and glanced up at us. "You two are private investigators?"

"We are. But we are here on personal business. However, we will be looking into Grayson's disappearance."

"Of course." The man put the card in his wallet. "If I hear anything, I'll let you know."

One of the officers stepped from Grayson's apartment. I'd decided to keep the information about the jump drive quiet —for now, at least. The less people who knew about it, the better. As far as the police were concerned, Michael and I had just stopped by on a personal visit. That was all they needed to know.

And that's what we told them.

But the bad feeling in my gut continued to grow, as did my guilt.

We were far from seeing the end of this trouble. Even if the bad guys had this jump drive now, that didn't mean that they were going to leave me alone. For all they knew, I could have a second copy.

And then there was the flip side of the coin.

This wasn't just about these guys harassing me.

I had my own determination to find answers. I wasn't going to stop until I knew what information my dad had been hiding. These guys weren't going to deter me.

I would do whatever it took to find out.

I prayed Grayson wasn't a casualty.

CHAPTER FOUR

"I HAVE a bad feeling about all this," I told Michael as we climbed back into his van. The parking garage seemed even darker around us now, more ominous. I halfway expected a getaway car to come barreling around the corner at any minute.

It didn't.

Michael's jaw remained tense. "Me too."

"I'm sorry I pulled your friend into this. If I had thought that he would be in danger . . ."

Michael turned to me, his gaze changing from angry to compassionate. "It's not your fault, Elliot."

"It feels like my fault. If I hadn't brought him the jump drive . . ." I squeezed my eyes shut, my thoughts pummeling me until I felt sore from the beating.

Michael reached forward, his fingers brushing my arm.

"There's no way these guys should have known we came here earlier. And Grayson wouldn't have just let them into his apartment. We're going to find out what happened."

"I hope so." I glanced down at my hands in my lap. "I just keep thinking this can't get worse, but it does."

"I want to come back later and see if we can look at the security footage," Michael said. "But we can't do that right now. The police are still on the scene—and maybe the CIA and FBI, given Grayson's career. I don't want them to know that we are investigating on our own."

"I'm not sure how someone could have gotten into that apartment complex and taken Grayson against his will without anyone seeing something." I kept trying to picture it playing out, but I couldn't. Grayson was a smart guy. He would have taken precautions.

"My guess is that they had a gun to his back and told Grayson if he made one wrong move he was going to die."

I shuddered at the brutality of it. Then again, I'd known these guys were heartless and determined—a lethal combination. "What can we do to find him besides looking at the security footage?"

Michael held up a set of keys in his hand. "We can look at his car."

"Where did you get those keys?"

"I found them near Grayson's desk."

Realization washed through me. Michael had taken them from his friend's apartment . . . I wasn't sure whether to pat his back or reprimand him. "Won't the police need them?"

"I'm sure the police will think of other ways to get into his car, especially if I leave it unlocked for them."

I couldn't argue that point, so I decided to move on. "What does his car look like?"

"That's what we need to figure out." Michael pulled out of his parking space and began driving. As he did, he hit the clicker on the keychain. He put our windows down, and the thick humid air from outside floated in.

The parking garage for the apartment complex was larger than one might think. Then again, the building was eight stories high so a lot of parking was needed.

I listened as we drove and as Michael continued to click the keys. Finally, as we reached the fourth level, I saw the lights flash on a car in the distance. Perfect.

Michael found a space, and we parked. Then we quickly ran over to Grayson's little red sports car.

I didn't know if there were going to be any clues inside. But it definitely couldn't hurt to look.

Michael grabbed something from his pocket and tossed it to me. "Put these on."

I glanced down to see some disposable gloves. "Really?"

"We don't want your prints to be found in his car. Believe me. And try not to disturb too many things. What I mostly want to know is if there are any clues as to where he may be."

I climbed in the passenger seat and glanced around,

trying to pretend I was Grayson. But his car was as neat as Grayson had been. There wasn't even any dried grass or paper straw wrappers to be found. I opened his glove compartment and began to search through things there.

Nothing.

As I did that, Michael looked under the seats. Between the seats. On top of the seats.

Still nothing.

"How could someone possibly keep their car this clean?" I asked aloud.

"Grayson's neat. But this even surprises me. It's not like he was stuck at home all the time. He did like to go out when he wasn't working."

"You think somebody wiped this down?" Elliot asked.

"I think it's a possibility," Michael said. "I think the people we're dealing with here are professionals. And I don't think they left any clues behind that will let us find them."

"So how are we going to find Grayson? And what exactly are these guys planning to do with him?" I felt sick to my stomach as I said the words.

Michael glanced at me but didn't say anything.

If someone had wiped this down, that meant that they'd been inside this car. Had they been looking for the jump drive? It was a good possibility.

But what if there was more to it than that?

On a whim, I climbed from the car and lay on my back beside the car.

"What are you doing?" Michael asked.

"You said Grayson had to speak to us in person. Maybe . . ."

"Someone was listening to his calls?" Michael finished.

"Yes, and, if that's the case, then maybe these people are also—"

"Tailing his every move?"

I snapped my fingers, loving it when we were in sync. "Yes!"

I reached under his wheel well and pulled something off. I showed the small device to Michael, whose face looked a little paler.

"A tracking device," he muttered.

"Exactly. Someone was onto Grayson. They may have even planted cameras in his apartment."

"And, if that's the case, they saw us in there. Overheard us talking."

My stomach sank.

This wasn't looking good.

"We need to leave this for the police to find," Michael said. "And then we need to check our own vehicles also."

MICHAEL and I arrived at the baseball field early. The sun was just beginning to sink lower in the distance and a pleasant spring breeze brushed over us.

The athletic park was nice—but that wasn't surprising considering this was Storm River.

The complex was located on the river, and there were probably eight different ball diamonds. On the other side, there were soccer fields, as well as some tennis courts and maybe even a Frisbee golf area. According to Michael, the Baby Kissers were practicing a few fields over from us. Since they were all politicians, I could only imagine they had security with them. Maybe American flags and cameras and unfulfilled promises as well.

A tribute to James Cruz had been set up near the field where we were practicing. Mostly, photos had been pinned to the fence, some candles and flowers left along the sidewalk, and a handwritten sign proclaiming, "Heaven Gained an All-Star." I wasn't sure who had left it, but the display was touching.

I stared at his picture for a moment. He'd had thick light-brown hair, a square jaw, and a smile that reminded me of a salesman about to close a deal.

I thought I'd heard his funeral would be on Friday. Certainly, there would be a big turnout for it.

Nobody else was here for practice yet, and they weren't expected to be here for another hour.

That was a good thing because Michael and I needed to get our act together. Discovering that Grayson was missing had thrown a wrench into those plans.

I had donned some black yoga pants and an official softball team shirt Michael had given me. Meanwhile, he wore his baseball pants and a Bigwigs jersey.

After we walked into the dugout and Michael dropped a bag full of bats and balls onto the ground, he turned to me.

"First things first," he started. "We're supposed to be dating."

My throat burned as I swallowed. "All right . . . although I'm still not sure why that's an important part of this undercover assignment."

"Oscar had a point when he said that nobody would believe us if we said you were involved in this for any other reason."

I crossed my arms and leveled my gaze. "So you're saying I don't look athletic?"

"It's not that you don't look athletic." Michael narrowed his eyes as he observed me. "It's that you don't *act* athletic."

"What's that supposed to mean?" I wasn't offended—I really wasn't.

He let his head fall to the side as he observed me. "What do you know about softball, Ms. Let's-Score-a-Touchdown?"

"Absolutely nothing. It seems like the most boring sport to ever grace society."

He pointed at me and clucked his tongue knowingly. "Exactly. That's why you get to play the part of girlfriend."

I offered a half eye roll.

"And speaking of playing the part of girlfriend."

Michael's voice swooped lower. "We're going to have to sell this. Are you ready for that?"

Something about the way his voice sounded made my throat tighten. "It depends on what you mean by *sell this*."

"I don't want to do anything to make you uncomfortable." He stepped closer and put a hand on my waist.

As he did, my skin seemed to burn at his touch.

I blinked, not expecting that reaction. Then again, I hadn't expected Michael to look at me like he was now either.

"Does it make you uncomfortable if I do this?" Michael murmured.

Did it make me uncomfortable? Was that how I would describe this feeling of fire burning through my skin?

No, I wasn't exactly uncomfortable. But something about it left me feeling off-balance, like a toucan that had eaten too many fermented berries.

"It's fine." My voice broke as I said the words.

"And if I hold your hand?" Michael moved his hand from my waist and grasped my fingers instead.

My throat tightened even more. I should not be having this reaction, but my body hadn't gotten that message.

His touch shouldn't shake me, nor should this moment make me. So why did I feel like something was awaking in me? It must be my earlier caffeine.

Okay, the last line didn't rhyme, but I couldn't think clearly right now.

"No problem," I finally choked out, trying to look more composed than I felt. "But that's probably as far as it should go. No kissing my cheek or smacking my butt or anything like that."

Humor raced through his gaze. "It's a deal. But somehow, you've got to not look quite as uncomfortable when I touch you."

I rubbed my throat. "I look uncomfortable?"

So much for my acting skills.

Michael let out a chuckle before abruptly stepping back. I instantly missed his closeness, missed the exhilaration of his touch.

Which was stupid. *Really* stupid. Michael was one of my closest friends—but that was all.

Michael observed me and nodded. "Yeah, you could definitely say that you look ill-at-ease. You look like you want to run. And that's a true fact."

Did I? Because I didn't really feel like I wanted to run. I really wasn't sure what I was feeling, other than confused.

"I can sell this." I raised my chin, determination echoing inside me. "I promise."

"Good. I look forward to seeing it. Now, we need to go over some of the basics of the game." He grabbed a clipboard where he had written out a few things for me.

I felt breathless at the sudden change.

I tried to focus. I hadn't been deprived of romance for so

long that I should feel so off-balance. So why was my heart racing right now?

"Do I really need to know these things?" I asked. "I mean, I am just the girlfriend. It's not like I'm going to be out there coaching."

"But if you were truly dating me, you would probably know some of these things. I just don't want you going into this totally green."

"Okay. I'll review this. And I'll be sitting in the dugout and cheering you on, just like the supportive girlfriend I am."

Michael nudged my chin with his finger. "I look forward to it."

I felt my cheeks heat and looked away.

What was going on with me? There was no reason for me to be reacting like this every time Michael looked at me or touched me.

I was going to have to figure out my crossed wires later.

Because a car had just pulled into the parking lot.

It was almost showtime. Or game time.

Scratch that. It was almost *practice* time.

Then again, I was going to have to put on a show if we wanted to win this game of finding a killer. So maybe it was all three.

CHAPTER FIVE

MICHAEL LOOKED RIGHT at home as he addressed all the players in the dugout.

As he should.

I still wasn't sure about everything that had happened to lead him to walk away from a career in professional baseball, yet he had. But Michael was obviously very comfortable here on the field. He paced like he owned this space, and he had everyone's rapt attention.

"I'm here today because of the unfortunate events leading to Coach Cruz's death," Michael said. "I know Coach Cruz would want all of us to put our best foot forward in order to win this game. Like it is every year, the Bigwigs vs. the Baby Kissers is a highlight for many in this area. Even though some of you have no prior experience with softball, we are here to make this a fun event for a good cause. Who's with me?"

Everyone cheered.

"I'd like to introduce you all to my 'assistant.'" He winked, and everyone chuckled. "Elliot, sweetie. Come up here with me."

Michael reached out his hand to me.

As I pushed myself from the chain-link fence where I'd been leaning, I shoved down the flutter of nerves and walked toward Michael. When I reached him, he slipped an arm around my waist as we faced all the players.

We were the picture of unity.

I hoped. Because, inside, I felt all off-balance.

I cleared my throat as I turned toward the team. "I look forward to rehearsing with you all."

Everyone laughed.

What had I said? Heat climbed up my cheeks.

Michael leaned closer and whispered, "Practice. We practice, not rehearse."

I swallowed hard. "I mean practice, of course."

"Elliot's going to be helping out with some logistics for the event," Michael continued, not missing a beat. "And if you have any questions, I know she'd be more than happy to answer them for you. Right, sweetie?"

"Just don't ask me about American softball terms." I kept my voice purposefully self-deprecating. My dad had taught me the art of deflection when I'd been bullied in middle school. Laugh with people, and it takes away their power.

Everyone chuckled again.

He let his arm trail from around my waist until it reached my hand. He brought it to his lips for a quick kiss. "She's brilliant, folks. Just be patient with the cultural differences."

My cheeks heated again. His words sounded so sincere, like he truly did believe in me despite all the mistakes I'd made since I entered this line of work.

"Now, I'm done talking." Michael clapped his hands. "Let's get on the field and start practicing."

I was so thankful I wasn't going to have to be on the field for this. Like so *so* thankful.

Balls flying at me at a high speed when I had no hand-eye coordination? It was the stuff of nightmares.

Instead, I took my place in the dugout so I could sit back and watch everything happen. So I could look for anyone who might be acting suspiciously. And so I could do what I did best.

And that was thinking. I *loved* to think.

I pretended to stare at the clipboard, which had the roster of all the players' names on it. But all I could really think about was whether somebody on this list was guilty of killing the coach.

That's what Michael and I needed to find out.

We planned to meet with Wally Winders ourselves so he

could tell us why exactly he thought the coach had been killed.

For now, I was going to watch for any signs of guilt from these players.

This event was like the Who's Who of Storm River. In fact, I recognized several of the faces.

Peter Harrington played first base. The wealthy man owned several businesses in town. The two of us had multiple encounters, but I had to admit the man seemed nice enough—in a snooty kind of way.

I also recognize the owner of Madison's Motors, a local car dealership. He and his team had recently taken home first place at the lip-synching competition. Larry "Lollipop" Reynolds. Apparently, he'd been given that nickname because he used to hand out lollipops to kids. It was kind of like baby kissing, I supposed.

A surgeon from that same lip-synching competition was also playing. Darren Cummings was in his early fifties yet his skin was still taut—a little too taut. Job perk, maybe?

Mischa Harrington was in the outfield. She was Peter Harrington's daughter and someone most people might call a socialite. I wasn't sure if she actually worked or if she just lived off her father's money.

Other team members included country club owner Royce Newton, Oleander Resort general manager Palmer Birmingham, and textile company president Ronald Backus.

I looked up as someone new pulled up to the field.

My breath caught.

It was Jono Harris, a man I'd gone on one date with . . . and who I suspected might be connected with the new regime that had taken over in Yerba.

What was he doing here?

Please tell me he wasn't playing . . .

I closed my eyes as I waited to see if my wish would come true.

A FEW MINUTES LATER, Jono dropped his bag in the dugout.

Wish failed.

"Elle?" Jono asked, his thick eyebrows pushed together.

That's what he called me. Probably because that's how I introduced myself when we first formally met. I'd been undercover.

The man had flashy good looks, with his gelled dark hair, tanned skin, and expensive clothing. No one could deny he was handsome—and he knew it. Jono was what was known as a "player"—and I wasn't talking about softball.

"You're not on the roster." It wasn't the most eloquent thing I could say, but my surprise superseded my courtesy.

"I'm filling in." He paused beside me and observed me for a moment, not bothering to hide his curiosity. "My dad was supposed to play, but he got called out of town on a business trip. How about you? You're . . . playing?"

He hardly knew me, yet he seemed to know I wasn't cut out for this. "No . . . I'm just . . . helping."

Jono and I had an interesting relationship. The first time I'd seen him, he had said some words in Spanish—the same warning words my father used to say. That put Jono at the top of my suspect list.

But if he was somehow involved in my father's death, I had no idea how. Jono was a rich playboy who liked to change girlfriends as frequently as some people changed underwear. Maybe more often.

I'd gone out with him a couple of weeks ago. It had gone well, I suppose. In fact, this Wednesday we were supposed to meet for a social after a local golf tournament. I had just texted him a couple of days ago agreeing to do so.

Of course, all of that was before I knew I was supposed to pretend to be Michael's girlfriend. What a can of caterpillars that had been opened . . .

My stomach twisted. How was I going to get out of this one?

The only reason I had agreed to go with Jono was because I'd wanted to find out for sure if the man knew my father or not. I was tired of dancing around the fire, and I figured attending the social with him might be the best way to gain some answers.

But now I found myself in this predicament, and I didn't

like it. I felt as if I was caught between an anaconda and a pit viper.

"Well, I think it's great that you're here." Jono flashed his movie star smile. "You're an interesting girl, Elle."

"I've been told that before." Though I wasn't sure it had been a compliment.

His gaze shifted, and his voice turned serious. "I had fun at our dinner date. It was nice. I've been thinking about you. In fact, I saw you at the Oleander lip-synching last week. You looked fine in that leather jacket and boots."

I stared at him, my eyes narrowing with confusion. "Of course I'm fine. Should I not be okay?"

He opened his mouth as if to say something but paused. People did that a lot around me.

"It means good. It means you looked good. Really good."

"Oh." Now it made more sense, I supposed.

Jono took a step toward the field. "I better get out there, though. But I'll see you around."

I nodded. "That sounds good." I nearly stumbled over my words as I said them.

Jono jogged onto the field. As soon as Michael saw him, his face darkened with disapproval.

The two of them had some type of past neither had shared with me. But I was curious as to what had happened between the two of them. They seemed like night and day.

Michael was very slow to open up about his history. Every time he did, I felt honored that he trusted me enough to share. But would he ever trust me enough to open up completely?

Just as the thought crossed my mind, goosebumps popped up across my skin.

I turned and looked around.

The feeling was all too familiar. I'd felt like someone had been watching me the past several weeks.

As I glanced around me, I saw no one.

I shivered as I glanced back at the field.

I only wished I believed that was true.

CHAPTER SIX

HALFWAY THROUGH PRACTICE, Mischa Harrington hobbled toward the dugout. She'd been in the outfield during the scrimmage, as Michael had called it. But, as she had been running, she'd landed on her foot wrong.

She sat down beside me and examined her ankle, a sour expression on her face.

"You okay?" I asked. "I can run and get some ice for you."

"I'm fine. I just need to sit for a minute." As she rubbed her ankle, she observed me a moment. "I've met you before, haven't I?"

"I think we were at a fundraiser together once." I didn't mention the fact that I had "accidentally" spilled my drink all over one of her friends in order to talk to her.

"Well, I have to say, Michael Straley is quite the catch. I know a lot of women in this area who have tried to get him to take notice of them. All he seems to care about is his daughter."

"That's not a bad thing, right?"

She shrugged. "I guess it depends on what you want. If you want to settle down into that kind of life, that's great. But if you want to party and have a little fun? Not so much."

I admired Michael even more for his stance on making his family his first priority.

"I'm kind of surprised that he's filling in as coach, although I guess it makes sense. He was Mr. Hotshot Baseball Player, after all."

I reminded myself that I was supposed to be Michael's girlfriend so I couldn't act so clueless.

"I know he loves baseball," I finally settled on saying.

Mischa seemed to hardly hear me. "Back in the day, before his injury, he was really good. If you wanted to be with somebody who was all the talk around town, he was your guy."

I still didn't know the story behind his past, about his daughter, Chloe, and Chloe's mom and everything that had gone on with them. As with most things concerning Michael, I was waiting on his timing for him to tell me.

I realized this was a great opportunity to turn the tables and find out some information from Mischa concerning this case. Investigating Michael wasn't exactly on my list—but Coach Cruz was.

I cleared my throat. "So, you don't really seem like the softball type."

She let out a brutal laugh. "I'm not."

"So what made you want to play?"

A far-off look floated through her gaze. As soon as it had appeared, it was gone. "I like to challenge myself to do new things. I have to admit, the coach's death has shaken me up. I considered dropping out. My father told me that I should stay, though, that we couldn't afford to lose any players. He said this was the best way to honor Coach Cruz's memory."

"And do you agree?"

She remained silent a moment before nodding. "I think he would want all of us to keep playing. Not only would he want us to all keep playing, but he would want us to win."

"It really was a tragedy what happened to him. A car accident?" I shook my head. "What a shame."

"I know." Mischa frowned before nibbling on her bottom lip. "It just doesn't even seem right, does it?"

"Not everybody seems all that shaken up by it." That was my way of placing the worm on the hook and sinking it into the water.

"Most people here are pretty absorbed with themselves. Not everybody liked the coach, though."

That was the conversation I needed to have. "Really? I heard Coach Cruz was pretty well-liked in the area."

I was playing what Michael referred to as devil's advocate.

"I suppose most people did. But he had a strong personality, so people either liked him for that or they didn't. Plus, there's always politics involved when you live in Storm River. Always."

The way she said the words was like an ominous warning.

She didn't have to tell me that. I already knew that politics ruled this area. And I wasn't even talking about the government diplomacy that took place in the Washington, DC, area. There seemed to be this "I'll scratch your back if you scratch mine" mentality wherever you went. And it wasn't just about how qualified you were. It was about who you were and who you knew.

I wasn't a fan of that mindset. Not by any stretch of the imagination. But I supposed it happened wherever you went. The scale just seemed bigger here.

I wasn't sure. I still wrestled with all of it, especially after my time in Yerba and experiencing the heartbreaking political uprising there.

Before I could ask any more questions, Mischa stood. "I think I've sat long enough. It was good talking to you, but I'm going to get back out onto the field now."

"Okay, I'll see you at halftime."

She looked back at me and narrowed her eyes, as if confused. And then she jogged back onto the field.

But I couldn't stop thinking about what she had told me. *Not everybody liked the coach.*

I needed to figure out who those people were.

BY THE TIME practice was over, I was covered with a thin layer of orange dust, another thin layer of sweat, and an enormous layer of boredom—one that was thick enough to smother me.

Softball just wasn't my sport. None of them were, for that matter.

The good news was that the sun was beginning to set, and the sky almost looked like cotton candy in the distance. The earthy scent of the river floated around us, as did the sounds of a Little League team practicing in the next field over.

As Michael walked toward me, I couldn't wait to hear his thoughts about tonight. Not that anything major had happened, but he had a good instinct for people. I wanted to know what he thought about this team.

However, just as he reached me, another man wearing a softball uniform wandered up to us.

"Coach Beasley," Michael said. "You're crossing into enemy territory."

What did that mean?

The coach, who appeared to be in his thirties, boasted a bright white smile—almost too white to be natural—paused beside us. "I just wanted to say welcome to the craziness."

"This is Elliot. Elliot, this is Coach Beasley. He coaches the Baby Kissers."

Now it was beginning to make sense. I extended my hand to him, and he shook it. "Nice to meet you."

"You sure you didn't bite off more than you could chew?" Coach Beasley asked, turning back to Michael.

"I'm more than sure," Michael said, unflustered. "How are your practices going?"

Beasley smirked. "Wouldn't you like to know?"

"Some of your players are up for reelection this year," Michael said. "It has to be a big distraction during your practices."

"Some of your guys have seen their stocks plummet lately. I'm sure that has to be an obstruction too."

I was pretty sure they were doing what was commonly referred to here in America as trash talking. I didn't quite understand it, but it seemed people enjoyed it.

"I just wanted to wish you the best of luck," Beasley said. "You're going to need it."

Before Michael could respond, a little boy from the Little League practice wandered over and tugged at Michael's shirt. "Didn't you used to play for the Mets?"

Michael knelt down beside him to look him in the eye. "I sure did."

He held out a baseball card. "I have been hoping I would run into you. Could I get your autograph? Please?"

The boy's mom stood beside him. "He's telling the truth.

He followed your career from day one, and he cried when you had to stop playing. When he heard you were coaching . . . he grabbed his card, just hoping he could meet you."

Michael flashed a grin at the boy. "I would love to sign this card for you. Do you have a pen?"

As their conversation continued, I glanced at Coach Beasley. He gave Michael a dirty look before wandering away.

Beasley was certainly an interesting character.

Then again, everyone here in Storm River was.

CHAPTER SEVEN

AFTER ALL THE PLAYERS LEFT, Michael came over and sat beside me on the dugout bench. "So, what did you think?"

"I think it's a good thing I'm not playing."

His lips tugged up in a smile that quickly disappeared, as if he thought better of it. "I think we've established that."

"I also think the outfield could be spread out a little more, especially on the right side. There's more open space on the left, which could be a disadvantage . . ."

"I'll keep that in mind. However, I was really asking about our pool of suspects."

Of course, that's what he'd meant. I tried to focus my thoughts. The air had turned cooler, but the sun still hadn't completely set. As summer got closer, the days were longer. I welcomed the change.

I sat up straighter and turned toward him. "I'm a tad confused as to why it has to be somebody on this team who potentially killed the coach. How did this Wally guy make that association? Just because the threats were centered around these practices?"

Michael shrugged, looking as laid-back as ever. The sunlight coming over the river washed his face in an orange color and made his eyes seem even more striking. Every part of him seemed tough, from his muscles to his tattoos. Yet, on the inside, he was like a pygmy marmoset—all cute, soft, and warm.

"It's not clear to me. Then again, we don't always ask questions. We take the case and let the evidence speak for itself."

"As far as I'm concerned, the evidence is as quiet as a snoop buried six feet under."

"What?"

I shook my head. "It's a Yerbian expression. Anyway, what if this really was just an accident?"

He released a long, slow breath. "We're going to meet with Wally tomorrow. Maybe we can figure it out then."

"Right. Maybe. In the meantime, I did have a few observations."

"Spill them." Michael turned toward me, all his attention on me—to the point I felt a little flushed.

Which was weird.

Maybe I needed some water. That had to be it.

"Two of our players were whispering to each other—a lot," I started.

"Which ones?"

"Lollipop Reynolds and Darren Cummings."

Michael nodded. "I noticed that too. However, the two are old friends. They could have just been gossiping. Men prefer to call that 'discussing things.' But same smell."

"I also observed Mischa stopping by the shrine. She looked really sad as she stared at the pictures."

"Good to know," Michael said. "That could have been for show. She does like her attention—especially when her dad is close by."

That made sense, based on what I knew about the woman. "And one man looked away when you talked about Coach Cruz, as if he didn't care. Rex Stephens of Stephens Investments."

"Good observations, Padawan. We'll dig deeper tomorrow."

"Padawan?"

"*Star Wars*?" He squinted. "You have seen *Star Wars*, haven't you?"

I shook my head. "I've heard of it . . ."

"I'm going to have to change that. And soon."

I licked my lips as I prepared to change the subject. "So we go back to Grayson's apartment complex now?"

Michael glanced at me, his eyebrows shooting in the air. "Now?"

"I mean, there's no time like the present, right?" I was anxious to find answers, and I figured he would be also.

"I would but . . . I've got to get home to Chloe." Underlying apology lined his voice.

My heart sank, even though I totally understood. "Of course. It's just . . . with working during the day and doing this at night, it's not going to leave us a lot of time to look into Grayson."

I just couldn't get that situation out of my mind—the feeling that vital information was now gone. The fact that I'd put Grayson in danger. The realization that this was far from being over.

"I know. And I know you're worried about this. But we'll look into it." His gaze met mine and promises stretched there. "Besides, the CIA and FBI will be all over this. We don't want them scrutinizing us—not unless you want to explain your father's secret career to them."

I couldn't argue with that.

"And what about the Beltway Killer?" I wasn't sure where the question had come from.

Certainly, I had enough other worries on my mind. But I couldn't stop thinking about his latest victim. Nor could I stop thinking about who might be next.

A chill washed through me at the thought.

Something changed in Michael's gaze. Concern filled his eyes, and he frowned. "It's definitely unsettling to think about. Maybe I should follow you home tonight, just in case."

I shook my head. "No, that's not what I was hinting at. It just seems like there's a lot going on, and I'm having trouble focusing. I want to fix everything and find all the answers."

"That's understandable. Just be patient. Things will come together." Michael stood, looking both tired and invigorated at the same time.

He loved baseball, didn't he? The exhaustion that came after doing something that fulfilled you was the best kind of tired you could be.

I suppose I could understand. I'd never seen myself being an investigator. But now that I had started, the job seemed to have gotten into my blood.

That's why I knew exactly what I needed to do tonight.

After Michael drove me back to the office to get my car and I waved goodbye to him, I headed toward Grayson's apartment building.

I was going to talk to the security at Grayson's building myself.

Because this was personal. I couldn't bear the thought of Grayson getting hurt because of me. And if I wanted to find my father's killer, then I needed that jump drive.

AS I WALKED into Grayson's apartment building, my mind ran through everything Michael had taught me in this line of work.

Sometimes you had to take each situation as it came. Some situations called for you to look tough and aggressive. In other situations it helped if you looked innocent and clueless. There was an art to prying into other people's business.

Until I met the security guard and saw his face, I wasn't sure which direction I needed to go. I prayed for wisdom as I made that choice.

Then I wondered how God felt about me praying about the possibility of lying.

I let out a sigh, recognizing the familiar struggle.

I ambled toward an office off of the main entrance. A sign on the door read "Night Manager." I peered inside and saw a woman staring at her computer. As she glanced up, I plastered on my biggest smile.

"Hey there," I started. "I'm Elliot. I'm a private investigator, and I'm looking into the disappearance of one of your residents. I'm hoping I can see some security footage."

The woman, who had to be around my age, stared at me for a moment as if my appearance surprised her. "Do you have a warrant?"

I shook my head and shrugged, trying to remain friendly. "No, private investigators can't get warrants."

She practically smirked. "Then I'm sure there's some type of privacy that won't allow us to show just any old Joe off the street that footage."

Any old Joe? Was that another Americanism that I didn't

understand? Apparently, it was. And who was Joe that he warranted the expression?

"I'm afraid this matter is very important." I tried to tap into my more professional persona. Flexibility was the name of the game here. "The man who disappeared is actually a personal friend as well, and we're extremely worried about him. Every moment counts if we're going to find him before it's too late."

Her smile dimmed. "I understand that, but there are laws we need to follow."

"Any of the camera footage you recorded would have been set up in a public area. Therefore, it's not private. There are no laws that you would be breaking." I wasn't 100 percent sure that my words were true, but I felt fairly certain I was correct.

She stared at me another moment, still looking uncertain. Then she picked up her phone, dialed, and muttered something into the mouthpiece. A moment later, a man who looked fresh out of high school appeared around the corner. He wore a security guard uniform but his eyes looked rather blank.

"Can I help you?" He paused in front of me, an almost dopey look on his face.

The little tag on his shirt read "George," but, for some reason, he seemed like more of an overgrown teenager to me than a professional. Maybe it was his oversized frame or his wide eyes or how he smiled a little too quickly.

I went through my whole spiel again about being a private investigator and needing to see the footage. I ended with, "Every minute counts here. We need to find out what happened to this man before it's too late. I know you want to do everything you can to help, right? What if he was your brother?"

"My brother?" His eyes widened even more. "I'd do anything for him."

I nodded, keeping my expression serious. "Exactly."

He hesitated another moment before nodding. "Okay. You're right. Justice is justice. Follow me, and I'll show you what I showed the police today."

My heart raced with excitement. This was good. I was making some headway.

I wasn't sure if Michael was going to approve of this or not, but I felt rather proud of myself—kind of like a peacock strutting his feathers like he was making an appearance at fashion week.

CHAPTER EIGHT

THE SECURITY GUARD and I went into a little room off the main office where TV screens had been set up.

"Let me pull up the footage," George said.

As he did that, I stared at the monitors in front of me. I studied the various camera angles, itching to adjust them so they weren't so off-centered and crooked. But I knew that wasn't the point. The point was to get as much of an angle as possible in different areas around the complex.

I was a little obsessed with symmetry sometimes, but I was considering taking some kind of class where I could go through twelve steps and get over it.

However, I knew that would never work. I loved order and balance. It was just the way God had made me.

Instead, I waited for the man to find the footage.

"Here it is." He pointed to one of the screens.

I leaned in closer so I could see. Sure enough, two men emerged from Grayson's apartment, pushing Grayson in front of them.

As they walked, something jutted from one of their jackets.

A gun, no doubt.

Michael was right. These guys had forced him out under coercion.

My heart thudded with regret.

Poor Grayson. What had I gotten him into?

The security guard switched to the camera that showed the men leading Grayson down the stairway and out into the parking garage.

Once they got there, the screen went black.

"What happened?" I sat on the edge of my seat, waiting to see what would happen next.

"They sprayed the garage camera," George said. "We can't see which car was theirs."

Disappointment swooped over me. "Weren't there other cameras in the parking garage that would have picked them up when they arrived?"

"They spray-painted them all. We believe the men parked on the first level, so it wasn't as big of a task as it might have sounded."

I frowned. "That's unfortunate."

"Yes, it is."

"Any chance I could take a video of the video?" I pulled out my phone in anticipation.

He cringed, his face scrunching with uncertainty. "I don't know . . . I think I could lose my job over that one."

"Really? Your boss would do that?"

"You would definitely need his approval first. I can't lose my job. I have two kids to feed, and I'm not even sure I should be showing you any of this."

That ended my pressuring him to help.

I frowned as I thought through my other options. What would Michael do?

Suddenly, I knew. "Can you play it for me one more time then?"

"Sure." He found the footage again and hit play.

As he did, I leaned on his desk and "accidentally" knocked over his pencil holder. The contents dropped all over the floor.

"Oh, I'm so sorry," I muttered.

"It's no problem."

As George leaned down to pick them up, I held up my phone and snapped a few pictures of the security footage. At least I'd have an image of those men who'd taken Grayson. It would be a start.

As soon as the guard picked up the last pencil, I flashed a smile at him. "Thank you for your help."

He nodded. "It's no problem. I hope you find your friend. And let's keep this meeting between us."

"It's a deal."

<hr>

AS I MEANDERED BACK to my car, my thoughts raced.

At least I had an image of the men who'd abducted Grayson. It was hard to tell much by the pictures because the kidnappers wore hats that obscured their faces from the cameras. But, best I could tell, they appeared to be men in their twenties or thirties who were relatively fit and thin. They were either Caucasian or Hispanic. The lighting made it hard to make out details.

As I thought it all through, I realized I really didn't know much more now than I had before I came. But seeing that video had confirmed that someone had indeed abducted Grayson.

I frowned as I pulled out my car keys.

My car didn't have a fancy clicker like many of the vehicles in this complex probably had. No, mine was a beat-up old Buick that was mostly gray except for one door that was red. It had looked like this when I'd bought it, but I was able to pay cash. Few things excited me more than being debt free. My sister called it the epitome of nerd-dom. I didn't care.

As my footsteps echoed in the hollow parking garage, I paused and glanced around.

Was that another set of footsteps I heard?

I scanned the dark area but didn't see anybody else.

That didn't stop the hair on my arms from rising and goosebumps from popping out all over my flesh.

Was I really hearing things?

I didn't think so. I'd been through this song and dance before.

I walked faster, desperately wishing I did have a clicker so I could get into my car faster. The last thing I wanted to do was to waste time unlocking my door. Based on the tremble rushing through me, that was a possibility.

What if the men who'd taken Grayson were here now? What if they were just watching and waiting for me to come?

Because I was the link to that jump drive. As far as those guys knew, I might know what was on the device. I could still be seen as a threat to them.

My thoughts didn't make me feel any better.

My steps slowed for a minute.

There was that sound again.

Another subtle thud.

It came from somewhere in this parking garage.

I scanned my surroundings, but I still didn't see anybody.

Did that mean this person was hiding? Were they coming down from another level and obscured from my sight?

I had no idea, but I didn't like this.

Maybe I should have waited until Michael could come with me. But I just didn't feel like this could wait.

I needed to know what happened to Grayson. That wasn't

just for Grayson's sake—even though he was the first priority. But this also concerned me and my family. I had to keep my mom and sister safe.

Just as I reached my car, a figure dressed in all black appeared from around the corner.

And he looked right at me.

CHAPTER NINE

I GASPED as I stared at the man.

As I gripped my keys, my hands began to tremble.

My keys slipped from my fingers.

Quickly, I scooped them from the garage floor and found my car key.

But when I looked back up, the man was nowhere to be seen.

Where had he gone?

I glanced around again, expecting to see him somewhere. Probably right behind me.

But I didn't see him anywhere.

Unease continued to grow in me.

Quickly, I stuck my key into the lock and opened my door. I barely managed to pull it out of the door as I scrambled into the driver's seat. My hand hit the lock.

Not wasting any more time, I jammed my key into the ignition and cranked my engine.

Or I tried to crank my ignition.

But my engine refused to turn over.

Not now!

Dear Lord, if there's ever been a time that I've needed You, it's now.

I tried again.

My car just let out a pathetic whine instead of starting.

I glanced in my rearview mirror.

I still didn't see that man. What kind of game was he playing?

I turned the key one more time. As I did, a rhyme formed in my head. It matched the tune of "Twinkle, Twinkle Little Star," a song my mom sang to me as a child.

Please, car. Please, car. Please, car start. Right now I have got to dart. Over yonder in this place, is a killer who's seen my face. Please, car. Please, car. Please, car start. If you would, you'd help my heart.

This time, the engine caught.

I threw my car into Reverse and backed out.

But my body was a trembling mess as I started to navigate the channel of the parking garage. I'd never liked these kinds of places, and I didn't think I ever would. They made me feel claustrophobic.

Even more so now that there was a psychopath in the space with me.

Was he going back to his car? Was he going to chase me to my home?

I had no idea. To be honest, I didn't even want to find out. I just wanted to get to someplace safe. Somewhere where I could breathe. Where I could try to sort all of this out.

But maybe that was asking too much. I was going on a ride right now that I had never asked to go on. Now I had no idea how to get off. In fact, I was pretty sure I wouldn't be able to disengage, even if I wanted to.

Finally, I eased out of the parking garage.

I glanced in my rearview mirror one more time. I still didn't see the man or any other cars coming after me.

Something wasn't fitting. This wasn't making sense to me.

That man had definitely been looking for me. Had been waiting for me. I was certain of it.

But if that was the case, then he wouldn't have just disappeared.

I continued from the parking garage and headed home, watching all around me as I did.

No mysterious cars appeared.

But I had a feeling that this was far from being over with.

I'd checked my car for a tracking device earlier. I hadn't found one.

But that didn't mean that someone wasn't following my every move.

"ELLIOT, why do you look so pale?"

My mom wasted no time scrutinizing me as soon as I walked into my house. I wanted to deny her words, but I knew there was no use. Mom had always had the uncanny ability to see right through me. It was her superpower.

She'd found out not long ago that I was working for a private investigator, and she wasn't thrilled with that news. But, again, I was twenty-seven years old, and I had to start making some decisions for myself.

Back in Yerba, I'd had my own place. My own career. My own life.

That all had changed when my family had moved here and when my father had died.

To be honest, there had been moments before we left Yerba when I'd been tempted to stay there and let my family come here without me. But I knew that my sister needed me. And I was uncomfortable with what I'd seen happening in the country as well.

Everything had been turned upside down. I still hadn't quite found my balance or my place here in Storm River, and I missed the self-assured woman I'd once been.

But there was one thing that I was certain of. As I navigated this new time in my life, I was going to grow. To become stronger. To become a better version of who I used to be. I just had to be a little more patient with myself.

I deposited my purse on the table and remembered my mom's question. "I'm fine."

"You don't look fine."

Speaking of not looking fine, my mom looked tired. Really tired. She'd always seemed so youthful, and people had often mistaken us for sisters. I wasn't sure if that would be the case anymore. The stress and pressure of life was beginning to wear on her.

"It was just a long day," I finally told Mama, pausing in the entry.

"You've had a lot of those lately." She crossed her arms, not letting me off that hook so easily—like any good mom would do.

"What can I say? It's nice to stay busy."

My mom should understand that. She stayed busy working two jobs. She taught English online several days a week, and she also worked at a drugstore. My sister went to high school and hung out with her friends. It was like we were all living under the same roof but going different directions.

I told myself that it was just a phase, and our schedules would eventually calm down. Right now, my mom and I were doing everything we could to raise money for my sister's upcoming lung transplant surgery. We had to stay focused on our priorities.

"How was your day, Mama?" I went into the kitchen to fix myself some tea and a sandwich. I hoped my hands didn't tremble as I did so. No doubt my mom would be able to see that happening and call me out.

"It was fine." She let out a long sigh as she followed behind me.

I knew this was never the way she'd seen her life turning out. She'd been a missionary, and her life's goal had been to teach other people about Jesus. Coming back to the States only to become a widow who worked at Earl's Pharmacy was never in her plan.

I wished I could fix that. I wished I could snap my fingers and make everything right. That I could bring my dad back to life, and he could answer my questions and give me one of his hugs. That my mom's eyes would still look bright and happy as she stared at my father and as she immersed herself in the community back in Yerba. That my sister would be surrounded by her old friends at their old hangouts before cystic fibrosis had begun to get the best of her.

It was just too bad that life didn't work like that. But we had no choice except to move forward.

And that's exactly what I was determined to do. I'd try not to feel sorry for myself in the process.

CHAPTER TEN

THE NEXT MORNING, I couldn't wait to show Michael what I had discovered. I had taken the investigative techniques he'd taught me and applied them to the situation. As a result, I now had a picture of the two men who had taken Grayson. Granted, it wasn't a great picture, but it was something.

We met in the office at 8:00 a.m. I slipped into my chair and set my travel mug on my desk. Everyone else in the area seemed to favor fancy coffees in disposable cups. I brought mine from home. It was a nerdy money saver, but there was no shame in that.

Then I held up my phone. "Guess what I have?"

Michael leaned back in his seat and took a sip of his Starbucks coffee. He still didn't look like he had quite woken up yet. His eyes drooped slightly. His motions were slow. Even his shirt—a black T with the picture of a square Earth—seemed wrinkled, like it needed a jolt of coffee also.

"What's that?"

"I have an image of the men who abducted Grayson." My voice lilted with excitement. "I took it when the security guard wasn't looking."

He glanced at me, his eyes narrowed in thought. He slowly took the phone from me and studied the image. As he did, I waited for a "good job."

Instead, he handed the phone back to me, his expression placid. I thought he'd be impressed, but his body language showed none of that. Why not?

"You should have waited for me," he muttered.

My bottom lip dropped. "Why? I was able to get the information on my own."

His eyes seemed to harden as he looked at me. "We're messing with dangerous guys here. You had no business going alone."

My lip dropped open even more. This was not the reaction I'd expected. "I was just trying to help us out. You were busy and couldn't go, but I wasn't."

"You need to think before you do things like this, Elliot." Michael stood and walked toward the door, closing it so Velma couldn't hear.

"I really don't understand . . ." I shrugged as I looked up at Michael. "I thought you would be happy."

He paused in front of me. "I'm never going to be happy if

you put yourself in a situation where you could be hurt. Do you understand that?"

"I wasn't trying to put myself in a situation where I could be hurt. I'm here right now, aren't I? I'm fine." I didn't bother to tell him about the whole incident in the parking garage. Maybe I would save that for another time when I didn't need to prove a point.

"But you didn't know what the outcome could have been. The men who took Grayson could have been waiting there for you. If just one thing had been different, you might not be here right now."

My shock turned into irritation. I crossed my arms over my chest as I stared at Michael, still in disbelief that he wasn't thanking me right now. "Maybe instead of concentrating on that you could concentrate on the image of these men that I found. Isn't that the most important thing?"

"Keeping you safe is the most important thing," Michael told me. "If something happens to you while you're investigating, that changes everything. Do you understand that?"

Michael was really serious. *Surprisingly* serious. This was the last thing I had expected. My pride in my accomplishment shriveled like a grape in the blistering sun.

I didn't say anything, but Michael continued to stare at me.

"Do you understand?" he repeated.

"Yes," I finally said, my voice clipped. "I understand."

But it pained me to say the words. I didn't consider myself

to be a proud person, but I was definitely feeling edgy and halfway insulted right now.

I knew where Michael was coming from. I knew I shouldn't be angered by his concern. But it didn't sit right with me either.

"We've got to go talk to Wally." Michael paced toward the door.

"We're not going to talk about this picture?" I mean, sure, he didn't approve of what I'd done. But was he going to dismiss this evidence also?

He shook his head. "I can't tell anything about those two men from that photo. Maybe the police or the CIA/FBI will have an easier time. But as far as I'm concerned, we don't know anything more now than we did yesterday."

My irritation was becoming something more akin to anger all the time. Why couldn't Michael just give me a pat on the back? Was it that hard?

Before I could say anything else, Michael twirled his key on his finger and headed toward the door. "Come on. Let's go."

Oh, great. I was going to sit in the minivan with him for the next twenty or so minutes as we drove to talk to Wally. That seemed just as much fun as wading through a leech-infested pond.

It looked like I was picking up on this American sarcasm a lot more quickly than I had ever imagined.

That was just great—and, yes, that was sarcasm again.

AS MICHAEL and I rode down the road, I didn't say anything. It was probably better that way. No doubt, the wrong words would leave my mouth. I was usually pretty good about controlling my anger. Sure, I struggled with emotions at times. But anger? Not so much.

Michael didn't try to say that much either. He drummed his fingers against the steering wheel on occasion.

I hated the awkwardness between us. Usually when Michael and I were together, it felt easy. I couldn't say that about just anybody. When things felt natural between you and somebody else it was a gift. Most relationships were a lot of work.

I was pretty sure this was our first fight. It was weird, and I didn't like it. But I wasn't sure if I was ready to try to fix it yet either. If I tried to, it would involve me apologizing for something I felt I shouldn't apologize for. Where was the authenticity in that?

Instead, I stayed quiet.

A few minutes later, we pulled up to Wally's house, and Michael put the van in Park. I reached for the door handle when Michael called my name. I froze before turning toward him and waiting.

He frowned as he stared at me. Some of the irritation had left his eyes, replaced with gentleness.

The look was so sincere that it made my throat tighten.

"Look, Elliot." His jaw flexed, as it always did when he was deep in thought. "I'm sorry if I sounded harsh back at the office."

Was that his idea of an apology? I remained quiet for a moment until I finally nodded to acknowledge I'd heard him.

"I meant it when I said I don't want to see you get hurt," he continued, no sound of humor in his voice. "On the surface, this line of work might seem dangerous, but it's usually not. It's just a lot of surveillance and research. But then there are other times . . . times when the stakes are high. When you have to weigh whether the risk is worth it or not."

I waited for him to get to his point.

He shifted. "You're still green at this, Elliot. Although you have good instincts, you still have a lot to learn. You're too trusting."

I wanted to argue with him. I really did. But I couldn't.

Because he was right.

The good news was that my dad had taught me self-defense, so when that naivety got me in trouble, at least I had a fighting chance to get myself out of it.

There was so much about the culture here that I was still naïve to. And I was the type who wanted to see the best in situations. But that probably wouldn't serve me well when I was dealing with killers.

"I just need you to promise me that you won't try to be a lone ranger," Michael said. "Having someone with you, someone who will watch your back, can mean the difference between life and death."

When he said it like that, it seemed to make a lot of sense. Did I want to admit it, though? The willful side of me didn't want to.

"Do you understand?" His voice sounded gentle, like he was trying really hard not to pick a fight.

I let out a breath and knew I needed to stop being as stubborn as an alpaca on a rainy day. "I understand. I was only trying to help."

"I know you were, Elliot." Michael offered a twisted smile. "Just run these things past me first next time."

"Okay."

His twisted smile turned into more of a half grin. "Okay. Let's go talk to Wally now."

As we started to walk toward the man's house, I realized that I already felt better. It was always good when you could put an end to a problem that had begun to fester before that fester turned into an all-out infection.

It was a Yerbian phrase and sounded much better in Spanish.

Now I anticipated hearing what Wally had to tell us.

CHAPTER ELEVEN

WALLY WINDERS OWNED a chain of gyms and was known in the area for being a philanthropist. From seeing his house, I would have never guessed that he was as wealthy as he apparently was.

The house was a simple two-story, oversized cottage-style building. The structure was located on the water, and a good deal of property surrounded it. However, most of the wealthy in this area had houses that looked more like trophies.

Wally's did not.

The man himself also seemed unassuming. He was on the shorter side and skinny. He wore thick glasses, and his dark hair was gelled back away from his face—not necessarily in a stylish way, but more in a practical way. He wore a polo shirt and khaki shorts along with boat shoes.

For the past ten years, he'd been the coordinator for this

annual softball game. He'd apparently grown up poor and had to use a local food bank regularly as a child and even into young adulthood. Eventually, his gyms became popular and began opening across the country, and he'd shifted into a new socioeconomic class.

"Thanks for coming," Wally said as we met in the front yard. "I understand that you have questions that you wanted to ask me yourselves?"

Though the man was small, he spoke with an authority that showed no one should underestimate him. His words were crisp, precise, and confident.

"We do," Michael said. "Thank you for your time."

"Why don't we sit on the back porch? I have some lemonade and blueberry scones in case you're hungry."

Blueberry scones? I could definitely go for one of those. I tried not to look too eager, however.

We followed him around the house.

My eyes widened when I saw the man's backyard. While the front of his house had looked simple, the backyard was a true space to entertain. Brick pavers surrounded a large outdoor fireplace. His covered deck had an outdoor kitchen and a ceiling fan. There was also a pool and a hot tub, not to mention the huge pier and boat house.

Maybe Wally Winders did have a little bit more of that trophy mentality than I'd given him credit for.

Despite that, I had to admit that sitting in the shade on his deck and looking at the water was rather peaceful.

I took the lemonade he served me and put a scone on a napkin so I could nibble on it as we talked. The pastry was good. Really good—not too dry, not too moist. That, when combined with the gentle sunlight, singing birds, and pleasant breeze off the river, made for an idyllic meeting.

"So what do you need to know?" Wally sat across from us, an arm casually draped across the rattan loveseat. His body language made it clear that this was his domain, his kingdom.

"I've seen all the information laid out." Michael shifted in his seat, looking like somebody who had just come by to chat instead of a hard-nosed investigator.

I admired his ability to seamlessly shift his personas to accommodate a situation. It was almost like he always knew just what to do. Wouldn't that be nice?

"But I really would like to know a bit more beyond those basic facts," Michael continued.

"Ask me anything. I'd be happy to tell you whatever I know. For that matter, I should let you know that James Cruz was a huge fan of yours, Michael. That playoff game where you caught the ball in the last inning . . ." Wally shook his head as if reliving the moment. "It was an incredible play."

My interest perked. Michael didn't talk about that part of his life very much, but I was curious about it. He really had been a big deal, hadn't he?

"I'm honored to hear that." Michael shifted. "But what I

would really like to know is why you think Cruz's car accident wasn't so accidental."

"Because James was a good driver," Wally said. "He wasn't the type who would answer his phone or look at a text while he was behind the wheel. One of his cousins died while texting and driving, so he was adamant that he would never do it."

"The police report shows that he texted somebody two minutes and thirty seconds before the accident," Michael said. "I questioned the officer at the scene, but he wouldn't tell me what the text said or who it had been to."

Wally frowned. "I know. I heard that. But I don't believe it."

It was a little hard to refute that evidence. If no one else was in the car, then James was the only one who could have sent it. However, I didn't want to insult the man's intelligence.

"Besides, he loved that car," Wally continued. "It was a Bugatti."

"I've never heard of those," I muttered.

"They're expensive," Michael explained before turning back to Wally. "Why are you so certain that it's somebody from the team who did this to him?"

Wally released a deep breath and shifted forward. "After the second practice, James began receiving some threatening texts. They basically told him he needed to quit, that he was doing an awful job, and that his team was going to be a laughingstock."

Somebody obviously was taking this game very seriously. It was beyond my comprehension why they might do that. But people went crazy for crazier things, I supposed—like the dancing turtle that supposedly only appeared every twenty years.

It was a Yerbian thing.

"Another time, someone let the air out of all his tires," Wally continued. "The equipment accidentally got left here overnight. All the bats were sawed in half and had to be replaced. The balls were left in a bucket of water and also had to be replaced. The new team jerseys mysteriously disappeared. It was like everything that could go wrong in this game was happening."

"At the same time, a lot of those things seem rather immature and childish," Michael said. "But not like serious threats. The other team could have done it to mess with his head."

"James was becoming more and more uneasy." Wally's face made it clear he was undeterred from his opinion. "I could see it on his face. It was obvious that whoever was behind these things was becoming unhinged. One of the windows at his house was smashed. He called the police about that one, and they said it was probably just some neighborhood kids who were up to no good."

I broke off another piece of the scone before asking, "Nothing was stolen from inside?"

"No, it was just the window that was broken."

"Where was he heading when he was in the accident?" Michael asked. "Do you have any idea?"

Wally frowned and swatted at an insect. "The last I heard he was going to a meeting. He didn't tell me who it was with or what it was about. And I didn't ask any questions. James just said that he hoped things got a little easier for him afterward."

"And you told the police all of this?" Michael clarified.

"I did. But they said that there was really nothing to investigate and that the car accident was an accident. I know the department has a lot going on right now with this Beltway Killer. But that doesn't mean they should ignore every other case."

"Is there anyone you suspect could be guilty?" I asked.

Michael had taught me that trick. Always leave that open-ended question, and sometimes you got your best leads that way.

"There is one person." Wally crossed and uncrossed his legs.

Michael and I both seemed to lean forward together as we waited for his response.

"Rex Stephens."

"Frank Stephens' son?" I knew Frank Stephens from a prior investigation.

"That's right. Rex's son, Rex Jr., played high school baseball when James was the coach. However, he wasn't very good and was constantly benched. Rex Sr. comes from a family of overachievers, and he didn't take well to that."

"So you think Rex Sr. would try to kill over that now?" I asked, unable to hide the disbelief from my voice.

"When it comes to politics and sports . . . I wouldn't put anything past anyone. If I had to point you in the right direction as to where to start, it would be with him."

"Good to know," Michael said.

Wally leveled his gaze with Michael and me. "But I do want to warn you. You should be careful. Because the person who's behind this might target anybody who's in charge of the team, not just James."

At the sound of his words, a shudder went down my spine.

It seemed like everywhere I turned, I was facing dangerous situations. Was there anywhere that I could consider safe?

I no longer knew the answer to that question . . . and that fact unnerved me.

***

"WHAT NOW?" I asked as we climbed back into Michael's minivan.

"Now, I'd like to run past one of my friend's places. He's a mechanic. I brought a copy of the accident report with me, and I'd like to have him take a look at it."

"That sounds like a good start," I said, pulling my seatbelt on. "This case seems messed up, doesn't it?"

"Most of our cases do."

He was going to get no argument from me there.

"The thing is, I was watching everybody last night at practice," I said. "I can't really see any of those people being a killer. I mean, most of them are wealthy. What do they care about a softball coach? They volunteered to play this game of their own free will."

"Things are rarely that simple."

I couldn't argue that. But . . . "I guess what bothers me the most about this case is trying to figure out a motive. That's what's not matching up."

"Once we start digging deeper, maybe it will start making more sense."

I glanced at Michael as we headed down the road, trying to get his read on the situation. "Are there any likely suspects in your mind?"

He remained quiet for a moment before shrugging. "It's really too early to say. But if James was intentionally killed, the person who did it wasn't exactly the cold-blooded killer type. He or she was somebody who wanted to send a very subtle message. If this person did tamper with the car, it's a sneaky way of killing somebody. Does that fit the MO of all the wealthy players on our team? I would say yes."

I had never looked at it that way, but now that Michael said it, I supposed it made sense.

A few minutes of silence fell. As it did, another thought entered my mind. Actually, it had never left. But I figured now would be a good time to bring it up.

"What are we going to do about Grayson, Michael?" I asked. "I know it's probably not on your mind right now, but it's on mine."

"Grayson is all I can think about." Michael frowned and ran a hand over his mouth. "He's my friend. I am worried sick about him, to be honest."

Surprise washed over me. I wouldn't have guessed that. Michael must be hiding all that worry behind his calm façade.

"Part of me wants to drop everything and try to find him," I said.

"These guys who took him . . . they're not the kind who are going to leave a trail. We could drop everything to find him, but I don't think it's going to do any good."

"So we do nothing?" Certainly that wasn't what he was implying.

"I didn't say that. We're just going to have to think of more creative ways to find him. I put in a follow-up call with the police department to see if they would tell me anything. I doubt they will."

I frowned. "The security guard said that the garage security cameras had been blacked out. They weren't able to pick up the vehicle or license plate."

"There could be other security cameras in the area that

may have picked it up. I have a feeling these guys didn't leave any fingerprints behind. And that picture that you showed me . . . those guys could be anyone. The images weren't clear enough to make out any features to ID them."

I frowned. That had been what I was afraid of.

"And we haven't even talked about the Beltway Killer," I murmured.

Michael stole a glance at me. "Little Miss Optimistic is going a little bit dark today, isn't she?"

"It's hard to be all that perky when there's so much bad that's going on." I hated to sound like such a downer but . . . how could I not?

"I can't argue that. I did hear that they released the name of the latest victim. Miranda Tantor."

I tried to imprint that name in my mind. "Do you know anything about her?"

"She was twenty-one. She worked at a restaurant here in Storm River. She was single. No family. And all the evidence points to the Beltway Killer."

I repressed a shudder. "That means if he holds true to form then somebody else will be abducted and murdered within the week."

"Right now I think everybody in this area knows that. It's hard to forget." Michael pulled up to an auto shop. "We're here. Now let's see if my friend can tell anything from this report."

CHAPTER TWELVE

WHILE MICHAEL and his friend chatted in the work bay, my phone buzzed. A smile spread across my face when I saw Hunter's name on my screen.

"Hey, there," I answered.

"How's it going today, Elliot?"

I started to tell him things were going okay, but then I stopped myself.

That wasn't exactly truthful. A lot had happened since I last talked to him, and I wondered if he was like Michael and if he would fuss at me for going to look at that video footage on my own.

I didn't know. But I really didn't want to risk being yelled at again today.

"We're still investigating the death of James Cruz," I said

instead. I turned away from Michael and leaned against the minivan, letting sunlight flood my face.

"Any good leads?"

"Unfortunately, no." I frowned, wishing I had something different to say.

"Listen, I hope we can get together again soon, Elliot," Hunter said. "Work is slammed right now, though."

I could only imagine that it was. "Whenever you're able. I'm here."

It was just as well with me. I was feeling pretty slammed right now too trying to find Grayson and do this softball game this weekend.

"Thanks for being so understanding."

"Of course." That was me. Understanding Elliot. That didn't always work in my favor, however. If I hadn't been so understanding of Sergio, I might have never had my heart broken.

As Michael walked back toward me, I told Hunter goodbye and slipped my phone back into my pocket.

"Well?" I asked, turning toward him.

He paused in front of me and readjusted his baseball cap. "My friend is going to study the report some more. But, based just on what he's seen on paper, he didn't notice anything suspicious. Of course, he would really need to see the car itself to form an accurate opinion, and that probably isn't going to happen."

"Maybe once he looks at the report a little more something will stand out to him." The optimistic side of me reared its head again, naïvely hoping for the best.

"Let's hope."

I glanced at Michael, who made no move to get back into the van. It was no wonder. Today was gorgeous, with temperatures in the low seventies and no humidity.

"What now?" I finally asked.

"Now we need to dig into each player's past and see if we can find out anything. Then we'll have a little break until practice tonight. Sound good?"

"Sounds like a plan." I just knew we needed what Michael had called a grand slam if we were going to win this one.

I WORKED at the office the next few hours, researching and finding anything I could on the players of the Bigwigs.

In fact, I put together dossiers on everyone so I could organize my findings. Maybe it was a little over the top, but it helped me to arrange my thoughts.

I glanced at the first page. Peter Harrington. Sixty-three. A native of Delaware. Owned several businesses in the area, including the Oleander Resort. Divorced.

I'd even included a headshot of the man that I'd found online.

The man seemed to keep popping up wherever I went.

But he didn't seem like a killer. He appeared too focused on his businesses to worry about things like that.

The next dossier I came to was for Jono Harris. He also seemed to pop up wherever I was. What would his motive for murder possibly be? He was thirty, had no job, no wife or kids. His only interests were chasing women and flexing his wealth to anyone nearby.

Next: Rex Stephens. Forty-two. Married. Though he started off in the insurance world doing IT, he now worked for his father, Frank Stephens, who owned an investment firm.

Wally had indicated Rex could be guilty. Just because his son didn't get to play much high school baseball didn't seem like a reason for murder, though.

Mischa Harrington was next. She was twenty-four. Had gone to an Ivy League college. She had worked for a while for her father, Peter.

Reni Boston was the only other unmarried female player. She was in her thirties and ran a sunglasses store down in the retail area.

Again, I couldn't see either of them as a killer. Besides, didn't women usually kill using poison or something?

I'd crossed paths with a few of the other players during various investigations since I'd started with Driscoll and Associates. But no matter what I found out about these people, I still had a hard time thinking that any of them had murdered James Cruz.

Finally, I looked away from the computer and rubbed my eyes. I could use a little break from my desk work—something that I would have never said a few months ago.

Michael turned toward me from his desk. "Did you discover anything interesting?"

"I can't say I did. You?"

He shook his head. "Nothing that really caught my eye. We can talk to Rex at practice tonight, but I think the motive is weak."

"Me too." I handed him a stack of papers. "But I did organize these for you. Yes, it's the epitome of geekiness, but I'm unashamed."

His eyebrows shot up as he thumbed through the file. "Wow, you did all this?"

I shrugged. "I thought it might help me see all the potential suspects more clearly."

"Kudos." He shuffled through the papers for a few more minutes before glancing at his watch. "We have a few hours until we need to be at practice. I think you should probably just go ahead and take the rest of the afternoon off."

I wasn't opposed to taking the time off. But if I did that, I wanted to look for Grayson. And if I looked for Grayson, I didn't want to get fussed at for doing so.

And that left me in an interesting position.

Before I could figure out a plan, Michael turned toward me. "I have an idea."

My interest perked. "What's that?"

"I was hoping we could go talk to your friend."

Something about the way he said "friend" put me on edge. "What friend would that be?"

"The former diplomat to Yerba."

"Blaine?"

Michael shrugged. "You never told me his name."

I sucked in a breath. Blaine Kingsley had been the US ambassador to Yerba. My father had known him.

"You want me to talk to him again?" My throat ached as I said the words.

"He might be the only one who has answers for us," Michael said. "He seems to be the only person you've found who actually has a clue about why your father might have died. That means he might be the only person who can help us find Grayson."

I thought about it a minute before shrugging. "Okay then. Let's see if he's home."

Michael stared at me another moment before nodding. "Let's go."

CHAPTER THIRTEEN

WE PULLED up to the stately house that Blaine Kingsley called home. I'd been here only one other time, and I honestly wasn't sure if I would be welcomed back or not. I definitely wasn't sure if I was welcome here with Michael at my side.

I wasn't going to turn my friend away. I needed someone else to help me navigate this mystery surrounding my father. I'd realized that I could no longer do it alone.

Blaine himself answered on the first knock, and when he saw us, his eyes didn't even widen in surprise. It almost seemed like he was waiting for us to come.

"I see you brought a friend this time," he said, his voice formal.

The man had light-brown skin, a shock of dark hair, and a stocky build.

I introduced the two of them, and they exchanged curt nods before Blaine let us inside. His cats rubbed against my legs as soon as I walked in.

Blaine didn't offer to take me to his office this time. Instead, we stood in his entryway as he turned to address us. Based on his bathrobe, the soothing music in the background, and the smell of essential oils, I wondered if we'd interrupted a massage.

"What brings you by this time?" Blaine's voice was stiff and professional as he addressed us.

"I need to tell you something," I started. "I found a jump drive that belonged to my father. But it was stolen from the man who was trying to decrypt it."

Blaine winced, as if the words pained him. "I told you that you needed to be careful and keep a low profile."

"And I was. The person we gave it to was very trustworthy and reliable. But he's been abducted, along with the jump drive."

Blaine broke out of his stupor and shook his head. His hands went to his hips, and he looked away for a minute, as if gathering his thoughts.

"You have no idea what's on it?" he asked when he finally looked at me again.

"I don't. I was hoping that the person who was abducted could help me crack the code so we could see what was on it."

"I doubt you'll ever get it back now." He shook his head,

the action making it clear I'd made a huge mistake. "I wish you'd brought it to me, Elliot."

I had considered that. I didn't exactly know whom I could trust with this information. If I trusted the wrong person, everything could backfire. I wasn't even sure I should be telling him as much as I was now.

"Do you have any idea who may have taken him?" I asked. It was clear he knew things that I didn't. But he wasn't forthcoming with that information.

His lips twitched ever so slightly. "Sleeper agents who are a part of the new regime are scattered across this country. But mostly in this area. It could be anyone. I know the government has been trying to narrow down who these operatives may be. They're not necessarily trying to destroy the American way. But they are still working to destroy Yerba. The United States has always had good relations with that country, and most people here would agree that it would be beneficial to keep things that way."

"So people in the US government know about this?" I asked. Did that mean that Grayson had also known about it when we gave him that jump drive?

I had too many questions. Too many things that didn't make sense.

"If we were to look for him somewhere, do you know where that might be?" Michael stepped closer to me, as if to let me know he was on my side.

Good. I desperately needed to feel *someone* was on my side.

"I wish I could tell you. But I have no idea. I tried to warn you that these men were deadly. Tried to tell you that you should stay out of it." Blaine narrowed his gaze, almost as if this whole conversation annoyed him.

"How can I just walk away if one of these men may have murdered my father?" Did I really have to spell it out for him? The man was intelligent. Certainly he could put together the implications of this whole thing.

Blaine's expression didn't soften. "I don't know. But if you want to stay alive then you are going to need to leave this alone."

I didn't like the sound of his words. But maybe he told the truth. Maybe I should just back off.

The problem was, I couldn't see myself doing that.

***

MICHAEL and I arrived at the baseball field early. We'd brought clothes to change into at the public bathroom. Me, into my black leggings and baseball top. Michael, into his baseball jersey and whistle.

I had to admit that Michael looked really good in his baseball attire. Like a natural.

After depositing the equipment on the field, Michael

studied the clipboard and reviewed what we needed to do tonight. My job as Michael's "assistant" was to set up the bases and the rest of the equipment.

When I finished, I wandered into the dugout to sit in the shade for a minute and drink some water. As soon as I stepped inside, I saw something on the bench.

I walked over toward it and frowned.

I started to reach for the object, but I stopped myself.

It was a rose with a rope that had been tied like a noose around the stem.

Something flashed back into my mind. I went back in time to when I was eating with Hunter. And I remembered that phone call that he had gotten and the one-sided conversation.

He'd definitely mentioned something about a rose and a knot.

My impression had been that he had been talking about the Beltway Killer.

Panic began to scream through me.

Was I overthinking this? Was I assuming things that I shouldn't assume?

Or was this the calling card of the Beltway Killer?

And if that psycho had left this here . . . whom had it been for?

I suddenly felt as if I couldn't breathe. I rushed out into the field just as Michael was walking toward the dugout.

He caught my arms. "Whoa. Where's the fire?"

"Michael," I gasped, my head spinning.

His eyes narrowed as he realized that I wasn't playing right now. "What's wrong?"

I looked back at the bench and the rose there.

Slowly, I pointed. "That. That's what's wrong."

CHAPTER FOURTEEN

"YOU THINK the Beltway Killer left that?" Michael repeated, glancing at the rose.

"I do. But I don't know that." I rubbed my hand through my hair, trying to clear my thoughts. It was no use. My brain was too scrambled right now.

"Tell me again why you think this," Michael said, his voice irritatingly calm.

"It's just something I overheard Hunter saying." What if the Beltway Killer was here right now? What if he was watching our conversation?

My head spun even faster, and my lungs tightened as panic squeezed in.

"Even if you understood Hunter correctly, why would someone leave this here?" Michael continued. "What sense would it make?"

"I'm not sure what the killer does with the rose and knot. Does he leave it for his potential victims? Does he leave it on their bodies? I have no clue." My words came out too fast, but I couldn't stop them.

Michael held onto my arm as if he feared I might pass out. "Maybe you should call Hunter."

"And tell him that I overheard his conversation?" Did Michael understand the implications of that? I was going to look nosy and assuming. And what if I was wrong?

"It's not like you were trying to overhear. You just happened to. He'll understand."

Yeah, just like Michael had understood when I'd watched that security footage without him. Dread pooled in my gut.

I let out a long breath. I knew I needed to do something soon before people got here for practice. I didn't have time to agonize over my decision too long.

After another moment of hesitation, I pulled out my phone and dialed Hunter's number. He answered on the first ring.

His voice sounded so warm and friendly that I hated to burst his bubble. "Hunter, there's something that I think you need to see."

Hunter arrived at the scene ten minutes later. I met him at his car so I could explain everything before he got to the dugout. Meanwhile, Michael stayed nearby so nothing would happen to the potential evidence.

We were just in time because I saw Mr. Harrington, as well as Jono, pull into the lot.

"I wasn't trying to overhear anything," I told Hunter. "I really wasn't."

A shadow fell over Hunter's face, but he didn't scold me. "That's on me, not you. I should have assumed you'd be listening. I need you to promise that you're going to keep this between you and me."

He glanced at me as we walked toward the dugout. His tie flapped over his shoulder in the breeze, and his shoes clacked on the pavement. Suddenly, I didn't feel like he was my friend. Instead, I was keenly aware that he was an officer of the law.

By contrast, my sneakers made no sound. My leggings were effortless. And the wind tugged the edges of my hair from the ponytail I'd pulled it back in.

"I told Michael what I heard," I admitted. "I'm sorry. But I had to talk it through with someone. I didn't know if I was overreacting."

His face tightened, and he paused, turning toward me. "I understand. But we haven't released this information on purpose, Elliot. We're trying to keep it under wraps. It's our ace card, so to speak."

I had no idea what that meant, but . . . "I won't tell anyone else. I promise. And I have a million questions that I want to ask that I know you probably cannot answer."

He didn't say anything for a minute, but his gaze seemed to scrutinize me. "I need you to show me this flower."

I led him onto the field. He nodded a stiff hello to Michael before we walked into the dugout. He paused when he stepped inside and frowned.

That's when I knew I was right. There was more to this.

That flower and rope were connected to the Beltway Killer.

"Who knew that you would be here?" Hunter's voice turned all professional as he turned to address me.

"Anybody who's been following this softball game should know that the game is this Saturday and that we have practice almost every night this week," Michael said, stepping up beside me.

"Who knows the two of you are helping?"

"The coordinator and everyone at practice yesterday—plus anyone they might have told," Michael said. "It wasn't exactly a secret."

Hunter rubbed his jaw and glanced at the rose again. "I'm going to need you guys to keep your team on the other side of this fence until I can have my team come in here and sweep the area for evidence."

"I understand," Michael said. "I'm going to see if we can move to the next field over. That way we can really stay out of your hair."

"See what you can do," Hunter said, slipping on some gloves and stepping closer to the rose.

"Elliot, can you stay here and make sure no one gets past this gate?" Michael asked me.

His laser-focused gaze latched onto mine, and I knew he was determined to get through to me, to make sure I was really listening. Was it that obvious that I was about five seconds away from going into shock?

I cleared my throat. "Of course."

As Michael wandered away and put the phone to his ear, I stood at the entrance of the dugout using my body to block anyone from coming inside.

Jono was the first person to walk over.

Wasn't this cozy? I had Michael, Hunter, and Jono all here.

I wasn't sure if any of them felt awkward, but *I* felt awkward.

"Hey, good-looking." Jono smiled, casting a fleeting glance at Michael's retreating figure. Confusion washed over his features.

Was he trying to make Michael jealous? To rub it in that the two of us had been on a date? I wasn't sure.

"Hello to you too," I told him, trying to sound casual.

I kept my arm across the dugout entrance so he couldn't get by. I wasn't exactly sure what to say. I didn't think Hunter wanted me to tell everybody that this was a potential crime scene, especially since he wanted to keep the rose thing under wraps.

"How's your day going?" Jono's gaze was focused fully on me, almost as if I was the only person in the world.

That was how he got so many dates. That and his good looks. And his money.

Okay, so he had a lot going for him. But he also had a lot that women needed to be cautious about.

Right now, I just needed to keep him talking. "It wasn't bad. How about you?"

"Took the boat out. It was nice. You should come sometime. You never did check out my yacht."

I glanced behind me and saw Hunter looking over at me. He'd obviously heard part of this conversation. Everybody knew what Jono did when he took women back to his yacht. It wasn't something I would repeat.

Before I could respond, Mr. Harrington joined us. I kept my arm right in place, even though he stared at me as if I'd lost my mind. I really needed Michael to figure out if we could use that other field or not because I made a terrible security guard.

"Hello, Elliot." Mr. Harrington paused in front of me, his bag slung over his shoulder and his practice uniform looking shiny and clean.

"Mr. Harrington." I nodded, acting more eloquent than I felt. I needed to take some pointers from Michael. Or maybe some acting classes. Or both.

"We seem to keep running into each other." He stared at the dugout, as if wondering why I wasn't letting him through.

I stayed strong, keeping my arm in place.

"Yes, we do." I searched for something else to say but came up with nothing. I didn't want to give away anything, and I feared that's exactly what I might do if I started talking.

Thankfully, Rex wandered over and began talking about investments with Mr. Harrington. That should distract the two of them for a while.

A few minutes later, Michael appeared on the sidewalk near the dugout and clapped his hands.

"Hey, everybody," Michael called. "We're going to need to use this field over here tonight. So why don't you all grab your things and go on over?" He pointed to the field beside us.

Jono and Mr. Harrington gave me one more questioning look before taking their bags and starting across the field.

I released a breath.

But I was far from being relieved.

I needed to know whether or not I was a target.

WHILE REX STEPHENS was waiting his turn to bat, I made my way toward him and leaned against the chain-link fence, trying to look casual.

"So, your father is Frank Stephens?" I started. "I met him not long ago. Seems like a great guy."

Rex narrowed his eyes as he glanced over at me. "Are we talking about the same guy?"

Okay, so maybe this conversation wasn't going *exactly* the way I thought it might.

"In other news . . . it's crazy to think about what happened to Coach Cruz, isn't it? I heard you guys went way back." It wasn't my best transition, but it was going to have to work.

Rex still looked annoyed, and his eyes narrowed even more.

Maybe he didn't realize it, but he was a lot more like his father than he might know.

"My kid played baseball under him." Rex scowled, as if bad memories were pummeling him.

"Back when Cruz was a coach at the high school, right? That's so exciting, especially since you were able to play for him also in this charity game. Life comes full circle sometimes, doesn't it?"

He let out a grunt. "He was a horrible coach."

"Then why did you decide to play for him?"

"My dad thinks this will be good for our business, so here I am. I played back when I was in high school also. I had the chance to play for college, but instead I decided to focus totally on my computer science degree. My dad said that I would never make it professionally anyway."

Ouch. That might have hurt.

"Did you and the coach ever hang out outside of baseball?"

"We didn't hang out at all. Look, I don't know what you're getting at, but the two of us weren't friends. I didn't hate the man. But we weren't buddy-buddy either."

"Why not?"

"He didn't let my kid play. Rex Jr. is just as good as any of those other guys. It's all about politics. Who you know. And who likes you. It was a crying shame. Especially when I saw my son's self-esteem go downhill as a result."

"That would be difficult," I said.

A few minutes passed, and I desperately wanted to find out whether or not Rex had an alibi for Saturday when the coach had his accident.

But I couldn't think of a single reason to bring it up that didn't sound suspicious.

Then, again, it seemed like this guy already thought I was flighty. At this point, what would it hurt just to let him confirm that fact?

"There was some beautiful weather this past weekend, wasn't there?"

He moved up and was next in line to warm up to bat. Speaking of batting, he gripped his bat right now, and I wondered how it would feel if someone used that as a weapon.

Not good.

"It was beautiful. I was at a wedding down in Virginia

Beach. The ceremony was on the ocean, and the sky was spectacular. Couldn't have asked for a better evening."

Well, I guess that ruled him out. If the man was in Virginia Beach—which should be easy enough to confirm—then he definitely wouldn't have been able to kill the coach.

Unless he'd cut the brake line earlier or hired someone else to do it. Until we knew exactly what had happened with Cruz's car, it would be hard to find our killer.

MICHAEL SAT down on the bench beside me after everybody else had left. We both took a few minutes to catch our breath and gather our thoughts.

What a day.

In the distance, fans cheered at a Little League game. The scent of hot dogs and french fries from the concession stand floated through the air. If it wasn't for everything that had happened, this would be the perfect slice of American life.

Yet nothing felt right.

"What are you thinking?" Michael finally asked.

I stared at the field in front of me and frowned. "I'm thinking about the basic profile of the average serial killer."

He narrowed his eyes and swatted at a fly. "Why are you thinking about that?"

I gave him a look. He knew exactly why I was thinking

about that. "That rose with the nautical knot across it has shaken me up."

"As it should." He frowned again and glanced back at the field, his motions heavy and burdened.

"The average serial killer is a white man who's more on the affluent side. We're sitting on a team right now full of white men who are more on the affluent side. Our killer could be someone on this team."

"Let me get this straight." Michael suddenly straightened. "You think somebody on this team killed James. And you also think that someone on this team could be the serial killer."

"What if it's one and the same?" I hardly wanted the question to leave my lips. But I couldn't stop thinking about it.

"That seems like too much of a coincidence." He shook his head, as if he couldn't believe me.

I offered a half-frown. Michael had me on that one. Just like a tiger didn't change its stripes, once a serial killer got his modus operandi down, it generally didn't change. At least not that much.

"This whole thing has me feeling out of sorts," I told him.

"Good. You should feel out of sorts. This whole situation is serious, and in more than one way."

I let out a sigh, and my head dropped back against the chain-link fence behind me, causing it to rattle. The sound grated my nerves. "Do any of the people on this team have any experience with mechanics? Auto mechanics?"

"I doubt that most of the guys on this team have ever looked under the hood of a car unless they were bragging about something. They're the type who hire people to do things for them."

A loud burst of cheering sounded in the distance. How I wished I could be part of such a carefree moment.

"If the killer is on this team, it's someone who hired someone to do his dirty work," Michael said. "I can't see anybody here tampering with the coach's car themselves."

"You're probably right. But what bothers me more is I can't figure out who in their right mind would have a motive for it and what that motive might be."

"That's been bugging me too," Michael agreed.

"Isn't the number one cause of murder money?"

"It is. Followed closely behind with love."

I nibbled on my bottom lip. "So maybe we should look at one of the women on the team?"

"It's doubtful. My bets would be on the money, especially in this town."

He was probably right. "I'm just not sure how we're going to get anywhere with this. Besides, James didn't have money. So I have trouble seeing someone killing him for that reason."

"No, he didn't have money, but maybe he was trying to get

money from somebody else," Michael suggested. "Maybe somebody felt like they needed to silence him."

"Even if it's true, how do we prove it?"

"That's a great question. That's exactly what we need to figure out. And in the meantime, we've got to watch our backs." Michael's voice left no room for question.

I couldn't agree with him more.

I stood and stretched my back. "I'll be careful. I promise. But, I know you need to get home to Chloe now. Enough talking, right?"

Michael followed my lead and pushed himself to his feet. "I do. She's been going over to a friend's house after school."

We slowly started walking toward the parking lot. "Are your mom and dad out of town again?"

"They're at another conference. Their speaking schedule has gotten busy lately. I think they would really like to get on the conference circuit."

"That sounds . . . exciting."

He shrugged. "Maybe. Listen, Elliot, promise me you'll be careful."

"I promise." My voice caught. Because I'd never heard Michael sound so worried.

And that scared me more than the rose and nautical knot did.

CHAPTER FIFTEEN

WHEN I GOT BACK to my car, I was surprised to see Hunter leaning against it, waiting for me.

Michael took a step away, although the action seemed hesitant. "I'll let you two talk."

"Okay, thanks. Good rehearsal. I mean practice. Good practice."

A thin grin graced Michael's lips as he waved.

I stepped toward Hunter and smiled, hoping he hadn't heard my mix-up. "What a surprise."

He smiled softly, but the worry didn't disappear from his eyes. "I thought I should follow you home."

"Because of the rose?" I almost didn't want to ask the question, but I had to.

He didn't bother to hide the apprehension from his face

as he looked at me. "It's just a safety precaution. Nothing to be worried about."

If it was nothing to be worried about then he wouldn't be here. But I kept that thought to myself and nodded, trying to show my appreciation.

"Thank you," I said. "I guess we should hit the road."

He nodded, looking as serious as ever.

A moment later, I was in my car heading toward home. Every time I glanced in my rearview mirror, Hunter was there, following right behind me.

I had to admit that I was glad he was. It did make me feel better to have a second set of eyes on everything around me, especially given what had happened lately.

I still wasn't 100 percent sure what it meant that the rose with a knot around it had been left at the field. But I knew it wasn't good.

Finally, a few minutes later, I pulled up to my house and put my car into Park in front of it. I wondered what Hunter would do. If he would pull up beside me and wave before heading back to work.

To my surprise, he climbed out also and began to walk with me toward the door.

"Would you like to come in for a minute?" I felt it was only polite to ask him, but I prayed he said no. I wasn't exactly ready to introduce him to my mom and sister.

"That's okay," he said. "You have a minute to sit?"

I nodded, relieved at his choice.

The two of us lowered ourselves on the front steps of my home, and I waited for whatever it was that Hunter had to say. Because I was certain that he had to say something. He was a very purposeful kind of guy.

"I NEED to tell you something that you can't tell anybody," Hunter said.

The tension in me tightened. "Okay."

His eyes looked troubled as he stared off into the distance. "That rose with a knot on it . . . it's always left right before the Beltway Killer strikes."

The tension in me seemed to leave in one big gush as my muscles felt like they turned to gelatin. Trembling gelatin.

Was that even a thing? Kind of like a gelatin earthquake maybe?

I would figure out my descriptors later. Right now, I just let Hunter's words wash over me.

"So the rose and the knot are found before the killer strikes?"

"He leaves it to let people know that he has a new target in mind."

The quaking gelatin in me remained. "He didn't know who was going to be at that field to find it."

"The thing is, he doesn't always leave it directly for that person. But he leaves it somewhere to indicate what his next strike might be. I'm not saying it's you. But it could be somebody else on the team or somebody affiliated with someone on the team. It's really hard to say."

"This has been left with all the other victims?" I almost didn't even want to ask that question. But I had to. Still, a dull hum sounded in my ears. I suddenly couldn't get enough air into my lungs, no matter how hard I tried.

"It's always left before the kill and then we always find one with the victim as well."

That must have been what I had heard when I had overheard that phone call.

"I don't like this, Hunter." I shivered. And then I couldn't stop shivering. And it didn't matter what I did, the trembles probably wouldn't stop. Not until I knew if I was safe, as well as the people I loved.

"None of us like this," Hunter said. "I'm going to make sure that I send a patrol past your house, though, just to keep an eye on things."

"The first two pairs of murders were about a week apart," I repeated. I told myself that several times, almost like I didn't want to forget it.

"That's correct. But you have to remember his MO. He usually picks a woman in her twenties who doesn't really have anybody."

"But Kate had you." I wanted to slap my hand over my mouth as soon as the words left my lips. Kate had been Hunter's fiancée. I knew he didn't like to talk about her.

But how did she fit the profile matching his other victims?

"When she was snatched, she was up here alone. I was in the process of getting my things moved this way. She essentially fit the profile. None of her family lived in this area."

I reached forward and squeezed his arm. "I'm sorry. I shouldn't have said that."

"It was a valid question." Hunter turned toward me, reaching for my arm and not letting go. "I don't want to see anything happen to you, Elliot. I know we're just getting to know each other and that we're taking things slowly. But . . . this guy is a monster. I don't want to see you in his clutches."

"Believe me, you're not the only one."

"You need to be careful. None of this going off on your own and definitely no going into dangerous places alone."

"I vow to do better." I raised my hand, ignoring that trip I had taken yesterday to get information on Grayson.

Before we could talk any more, the front door opened, and my mom stepped out.

"Elliot," she started, her eyes lighting with surprise. "And you have a friend with you . . ."

"Mama, this is Hunter. Hunter this is my mama."

My mom's face glowed, as it often did when I brought home a boy that met her approval. "It is so nice to meet you."

"Nice to meet you too."

"Come inside. Stay for a while. Have some tea."

"I would. I really appreciate the invitation. But, unfortunately, I have got to get back to work. I'm on the clock right now."

"On the clock?" My mom raised her eyebrows. "What exactly is it that you do, Hunter?"

I stepped closer to him. "He's a detective, Mama."

I wasn't sure if that was approval or disappointment that crossed her gaze. "I see. Well, I don't want to keep you from what it is that you need to do. But it was very nice to meet you."

"You as well." Hunter turned back to me. "Stay safe and we'll talk later, okay?"

I nodded. "Okay."

We both stood there awkwardly for a moment. It was like we didn't know if we should hug or if I expected him to kiss my cheek or what.

But after a few seconds of awkwardness, Hunter nodded and walked back to his car.

As soon as he was out of earshot, Mama turned to me. "He seems like a nice young man."

"He is."

"Why do I feel like there's a but in there?"

"There's no but in there."

My mom gave me one of her all-knowing looks. "Elliot, I think it would be great if you found somebody. Please, don't hold back for my sake."

Was I holding back because of my mom? I didn't think so. But who knew what was going on in my subconscious?

"I won't," I told her. "I promise. I just don't want to rush into anything. And neither does Hunter."

"I see. That's probably wise. For now, how about that tea? Ruth is inside, and we can all catch up. I want to hear all about your day."

But did she? I had a feeling that answer would be no.

I wasn't going to be able to bring up the rose or the nautical knot. Instead, I was going to have to keep things on the surface. I was going to have to talk about softball.

And that pained me more than I ever thought it would.

CHAPTER SIXTEEN

A POLICE CAR drove past as I stepped onto my porch the next morning.

It looked like Hunter had done exactly what he said and sent a patrol past my house to watch for signs of trouble. It did make me feel better. Then again, I would feel even better if I had a personally armed escort every moment of the day.

I'd hardly gotten any sleep last night as I'd pictured the Beltway Killer sneaking into my house. I'd envisioned him opening windows or picking the lock to my front door. I imagined my mom finding a rose with a nautical knot on my bed.

I shuddered at the thought.

But there was one other thing that bothered me. Hunter had said that it wasn't necessarily me this man was targeting.

It could be somebody else at the game or somebody affiliated with somebody at the game.

If that meant that my sister and mom were in danger, then I wouldn't be getting any sleep for a very long time. My only comfort was in knowing that they weren't in the right age group. Neither were in their twenties.

But that didn't mean that this guy wasn't a threat to them.

I glanced around as I walked to my car, but I saw no one.

That was a good sign, I supposed.

I climbed into my car and took off for work. Michael and I were going to meet at Driscoll and Associates to talk about our case.

Before I even walked in the front door, Michael met me outside. "Police found the car that was used to abduct Grayson."

My heart fluttered. "And?"

Michael frowned and lowered his voice. "Nothing was inside. Nothing except some blood."

My stomach clenched. "Blood . . . ?"

"I know it's not exactly what you want to hear, but I wanted to give you the update."

I crossed my arms and leaned against the building. "So these men took Grayson and the jump drive. They managed to escape and abandon that vehicle. Maybe they had another vehicle waiting for them?"

Michael ran a hand over his face. "It's a possibility. The

good news is that Grayson wasn't inside. That could mean that he is still alive. I hope so, at least."

I hoped so also.

I studied Michael's face for a moment. "How did you find all of this out?"

"The police called me last night to ask me some follow-up questions." He sounded weary as he said the words.

"Was the blood . . . was there a lot of it?" My throat burned as I asked the question. "Or was it just a little?"

It sounded morbid, but I had to know.

"It wasn't enough to lead the police to think that someone had died." Michael's words sounded grim, solemn.

"That's good news, I guess." My words sounded weak, even to my own ears.

He nodded slowly, as if resigning himself to the truth. "I just wanted to let you know that I haven't forgotten about it."

"Thank you. I appreciate that, Michael."

Michael stared down at me for a moment, almost as if there was something unspoken in his gaze. I didn't know what it was. But I figured he would tell me when he was ready.

"We should probably get back inside," he finally said. "We need to work on tracking down some of these suspects again."

"Absolutely. Let's get to work."

MICHAEL and I had been sitting at our desks, going through Coach Cruz's background and social media for any clues. We'd found very little that would help us—so far, at least. As far as I could tell, Cruz didn't even have a girlfriend.

"Elliot." Excitement raced through Michael's voice as he swiveled in his chair to face me. "We have another lead."

My heart raced. I would really love to hear some good news right about now. "What's that?"

"I just got an anonymous text from someone saying they saw Coach Beasley messing with Coach Cruz's car before he died."

Now *that* was interesting. "So maybe the other coach did it? Maybe he didn't even intend for Coach Cruz to die. Maybe he just wanted to sabotage the team a little bit to give the Baby Kissers a better chance to win."

Michael offered a half-shrug, making it clear he was unconvinced. "Again, I don't love that motive. It seems extreme. But you could be right. Maybe whoever was behind this never intended on Cruz dying. Maybe they just wanted to put him out of commission for a while."

"Why would someone leave that tip anonymously?" I leaned back and took another sip of my coffee. "It's not like they're going to be implicating themselves."

"My guess is that maybe they're on the other team and don't want to be called out as a traitor."

I nodded. Michael's theory made sense. "So what do we do now?"

"Now, we are going to go pay the coach a visit."

Coach Beasley owned a sporting goods business here in Storm River, from what I understood. It wasn't the largest one—that was Easton's. Beasley's was a little hole-in-the-wall place that also had a batting cage in the back.

But the good news was that we were going to be able to talk to him, and maybe we would find out some answers.

All we needed was one break.

Just one.

CHAPTER SEVENTEEN

"WELL, well, well . . . would you look what the cat dragged in," Coach Beasley muttered as Michael and I stepped into his store.

I looked at my feet. I didn't see any cats in here.

Michael shook his head. "Never mind. It's another American expression."

I should have figured.

Coach Beasley leaned on the checkout counter as he stared at us, looking rather bored. "So what brings you two by here? Trying to learn some trade secrets so you can win the game? Come to ask for my expert advice?"

"No, actually we have a couple of questions for you." Michael paused near the counter and leveled his gaze on Beasley. "We heard that you were messing with Coach Cruz's car before he died."

In three seconds flat, Beasley's face went at least six shades lighter and he straightened. "I don't know what you're talking about."

"We have a witness who disagrees," Michael continued. "This witness says that you were seen messing with his car."

Beasley shook his head and practically snorted. As his hand swiped through the air, it hit a bucket of ping-pong balls, and they rolled all over the store.

"That person's wrong," Beasley muttered, collecting the balls from the counter.

Michael angled his head, unshaken by Beasley's denial. "Why would someone say that if it wasn't true?"

"You need to ask that person, not me." Beasley's voice sounded defensive and edgy as he stared at us.

Michael stepped closer, his figure imposing, especially when he put his hands on his hips. "No, you're the one who needs to start explaining. If you had something to do with that vandalism, then maybe you also had something to do with Cruz's death."

I didn't think Beasley's face could go any whiter, but it did. "You don't know what you're talking about. I would never kill somebody. Besides, Cruz was in an accident."

"Some people believe that his brake line may have been tampered with. They're calling it a homicide."

"The police are looking into it?" Beasley looked truly stunned with his wide eyes and parted lips. He glanced around, as if to make sure none of his customers were overhearing this.

Michael shrugged. "Something like that. Now, do you want to explain or do you want me to get the police involved in this matter?"

"No, no, no." Beasley's words came out rushed, almost panicked. "It wasn't like that."

"Then what was it like?" Michael gave him a hard stare.

I didn't have to say a word, which was just great because I was enjoying watching this confrontation. Beasley was sweating while Michael remained as cool as a cucumber.

"I *may* have sabotaged some of your equipment. And I *may* have let the air out of his tires. That was as far as it went."

"And why would you do that?" Michael demanded.

"It was just some good, healthy competition. That's all."

"You were trying to sabotage the game, weren't you? Your own version of Deflategate."

Beasley leaned closer, his teeth clenched as he whispered, "I would never try to kill Cruz. This was all in good fun. The Baby Kissers just want to win, and we're trying to distract the other team. But nothing like that."

"So where were you on Saturday evening after practice?" Michael asked.

"I was at home with my wife and kids. We also had some family friends over. You can talk to them and they'll verify that I was nowhere near Coach Cruz or his car."

"Are you sure about that? Because if you aren't, I'm going to prove it." Michael's voice left no room for doubt.

"Talk to my wife. I know nothing about cars. The last time I tried to change my oil for myself, I forgot to put something back on and the oil leaked all over our driveway."

"I hope you're telling the truth," Michael warned. "But, if not, there will be consequences. The police will make sure of that."

CHAPTER EIGHTEEN

"HE'S A SNAKE," I muttered as we climbed into Michael's minivan.

Michael scowled as he clicked his seatbelt in place. "Yes, he is. Then again, that's not a surprise. You'd be surprised at the lengths people will go to win."

I wondered if there was more to his story.

Before I could ask, Michael continued, "I'd like to go see James Cruz's house now."

I glanced at him in surprise. "Do you have a key so we can get inside?"

"No. But we should still look at it. You never know what might pop out."

I didn't question him. Instead, we headed through town. Michael seemed to know just where he was going.

I wasn't sure exactly what kind of house I had expected

James Cruz to live in. In my mind, he was still a high school coach living on a teacher's salary. But I reminded myself that he was actually a consultant now for Wally's fitness centers.

That's why, when Michael and I pulled up to the large house with the manicured lawn, I shouldn't have been surprised.

But I was. Cruz's house was nice, even for Storm River. And that was saying a lot when you considered what a ritzy area this was.

As Michael parked across the street, I rolled down my window slightly to get a better look at the two-story place with its clean blue siding, multiple eaves, and inviting porch.

Were the answers waiting for us here?

Michael hopped out and motioned for me to follow.

"Where you going?" I asked, realizing I had no idea what our plan was.

"Let's check it out."

That didn't make much sense considering we didn't have a key or an opportunity to get inside. But I followed behind Michael anyway.

He walked across the front of the house before opening the gate and slipping into a fenced-in area instead. The backyard was just as manicured as the front and even had a pool and a hot tub.

Nice . . . this was how the other half lived. One would think I'd be used to seeing homes like this now.

Michael walked on the deck to the back door. He tugged on it but it didn't open.

That's when he pulled something out of his pocket.

"What are you doing?" I asked, watching closely.

"I want to see inside his house, sweetie."

"You don't have to call me that when no one is watching."

He winked. "But it's kind of fun to watch you get flustered. Plus, it's good practice. That's a true fact."

I ignored him. "Is this illegal?"

"Cruz isn't here to press charges now, is he?"

"Does he live with anyone?"

"Nope." He continued to fiddle with the lock.

A bad feeling gurgled in my stomach. This was the first time I'd actually broken into a place, and it made me feel a slight bit off-balance.

I wanted to recite the Lord's Prayer, but it seemed sacrilegious at a time like this.

After several minutes, the lock finally gave. Michael pushed the door open and stepped inside.

I swallowed hard and braced myself for whatever we might find inside.

***

THE INSIDE of Cruz's house matched the outside. Everything seemed to be in place, with no expense spared. The floors were wooden and glossy. The furniture leather. The countertops marble.

"Careful what you touch," Michael said as we paused in the kitchen. "Just in case the police ever decide to open this up as a homicide, we don't want to leave any evidence behind that we've been here. Nor do we want to mess anything up that would hinder their investigation."

"You act like you've done this before." I wasn't sure if that fact intrigued me or bothered me.

Michael didn't say anything, which I took to mean that he had.

"Let's stick together," Michael said. "Just to be on the safe side."

Did that mean that he thought somebody could be here? Or that somebody could possibly come in?

I didn't know, and I didn't ask.

I'm breaking into a house. It makes me feel like a louse. But we need the truth, and we need some proof, so I guess I can do this, though it's uncouth.

Instead, Michael tossed me some gloves. "Wear these, just in case."

It was a good thing he had such a handy supply of them.

We searched the downstairs of his house, looking for anything of note. We didn't see anything . . . until we reached the office.

I pulled open a drawer and found some bills there. As I

began to look through them, I noticed that most of them were overdue.

"What do you make of this?" I asked Michael, holding the papers up.

"It appears the coach may have been having some financial troubles." Michael held up another sheet of paper. "And it looks like he may have been considering selling this place."

I leaned closer for a better look. Sure enough, a realtor had done a comp sheet on other houses in the area.

"I wonder what happened?" Based on his house and car, Cruz was doing well for himself.

"That's what we need to figure out, I guess."

Michael pulled out his desk chair and sat at the computer. After he fiddled around for a few minutes, the computer screen popped on.

"How did you do that?" I muttered.

"It's usually not that hard to guess people's passwords."

He stared at the screen, hitting several buttons and moving so quickly I had no idea what he was doing.

Finally, he let out a grunt.

"What is it?" I asked, leaning closer.

"Thanks to his cloud account, I was able to access some of his text messages," Michael said, a certain amount of satisfaction in his voice.

"Anything interesting?" He should be proud. This could be the information we were looking for.

He pointed at the screen. "The text that was sent right

before his accident is to an unknown number. Cruz said, 'I can't take it anymore.' There were no texts before that."

I glanced at Michael, a new thought circling in my head. "You think he ran into that tree on purpose? Could that be why there were no skid marks?"

"That's a great question." Michael looked back at me and raised his eyebrows.

"I wonder who he was texting." I grabbed my phone and took a picture of the text, just in case we needed any of those details later.

"An unknown number?" Michael said. "Maybe it was a woman."

"Was he dating someone?" I hadn't heard anything about that as I'd questioned people, nor had I seen anything on his social media.

"Someone like Cruz? I would guess the answer is yes. Maybe no one seriously, but I bet he liked having some arm candy."

"Arm candy?"

"Someone pretty at his side."

Made sense, I supposed. The web kept getting more tangled, didn't it? Who did he send this text to? Why would someone who was adamantly against texting while driving send something like this? He must have felt it was important or urgent if he did so.

"Any other interesting texts?" I stared at the screen.

"It looks like there are some here to the realtor about

selling his house." He pointed to the screen. "That's all I see right now, other than some random texts about practice and work."

Movement out the front window caught my eye. A car parked on the street out front, and, a moment later, a man climbed out and walked toward Cruz's house.

Michael followed my gaze and straightened. "We need to get out of here. That's Cruz's brother, if I remember correctly. He's convinced Cruz's death was an accident. When I tried to talk to him earlier, he didn't seem at all interested."

Without asking any more questions, we took off toward the back door and slipped out just as the front door opened.

***

AFTER SNEAKING out the back and around the side of the house, I had to admit that I felt invigorated—and I had the strong urge to repent for that. Doing illegal things should *not* make me feel this excited.

I expected Michael to look and feel the same way. But as I glanced at him after we climbed back into his van, I noticed he looked pale and his eyes seemed glazed.

"You're not looking like you feel so great," I murmured.

Was he having regrets about going into Cruz's place? I didn't think so.

"I'm starting to feel a little achy for some reason," he muttered. "I'll be fine. It's probably just allergies."

I squinted as I examined him closer. His motions definitely seemed sluggish. "I don't know about that. Maybe you should go home and rest."

"Don't be silly. I'm fine."

"The good news is we don't have practice tonight," I reminded him.

No, tonight was the golf tournament that Jono had invited me to. The Who's Who of town would also be involved in the fundraiser. I had a feeling that's why there was no practice. Everyone would be at the tournament instead.

Around here, people's social lives seemed to carry just as much importance as their wallets.

"You're going?" Michael's voice rose in surprise—and maybe disappointment—as he turned to me in the van. We still sat near the curb, discussing our next options.

I frowned. "I am. I want to know what Jono knows about my dad. I'm tired of dancing around the fire, and I just need to ask him."

"Dancing around the fire?"

"You know, when you have a guinea pig to roast?"

"No, I have no idea what you're talking about. But are you sure that's a good idea?" His voice sounded strained.

I appreciated his concern. What did he think? That Jono was the Beltway Killer or something? "I won't be alone with him. I'll be surrounded by a lot of people."

"What about our cover?" Michael asked. "We're supposed to be dating . . . sweetie."

I frowned as I remembered what I'd told Jono. "I explained that we had a very open relationship."

Michael let out a chuckle and ran a hand over his face. "Did you?"

"I didn't know what else to say while keeping our cover." It was the first thing that popped out.

"I don't know what to tell you. But you definitely don't seem like the open relationship type of girl."

I crossed my arms. "I know, right? I'm totally not. I can't believe he fell for it."

"You might be surprised at what Jono would fall for."

I tilted my head. There it was again. Those hints about whatever it was that had happened between Michael and Jono. When would Michael ever trust me enough to open up about his past?

I didn't know. I suppose I just had to be grateful for the baby steps we'd already taken.

As I studied Michael's face again, I felt certain he was coming down with something.

"We should get going," I told him. "I need to get changed, and you need to get some rest. I'm sure Chloe will be a great nurse."

A small smile started at his lips as he put his van in Drive and we headed down the road. "I'm sure she will be. She likes to pretend like she's the boss of me."

I smiled as I pictured it. "She's a great girl."

We continued down the road until we pulled back up at the office. Michael had decided to not go inside. He was going to take my advice and go lie down.

Before I climbed out, I turned to Michael. "If you need anything, call me. You promise?"

"I promise." But his voice sounded lackluster. "Have fun at the golf tournament."

I'd rather be chased by an ocelot through the rainforest than play golf.

But I would do anything to find answers about my father. And that was the only reason I was going tonight. However, I would need to be on my A game.

AT FOUR O'CLOCK, I met Jono Harris at the Founder's Circle Golf and Country Club. I'd dressed in a cute little sundress that Velma had helped me pick out.

The good news was the weather was perfect for the event —the sun was shining, the humidity was low, and spring flowers added their fragrance to the air.

I ran my hand down the turquoise dress and pushed away my nerves as I stepped out onto the patio where people mingled with colorful drinks and dainty little plates of food. I recognized several people from around town, although hardly anyone gave me a second glance.

Coming here was a bad idea, wasn't it?

Maybe I could leave now and text Jono some kind of excuse. I didn't belong in this world.

No, this was a place for the Mischa Harringtons of society, not a missionary's kid with a beat-up car that looked like an exercise in "Which one of these things don't belong?" in the parking lot.

Before I could turn to go, someone stepped in front of me. Jono.

As expected, he looked dashing in his shorts and polo shirt.

His grin widened as he looked me up and down. "Elle, I'm so glad you could join me. You look wonderful, as always."

"Thanks for the invite. How did the game go?"

"My team won—of course." He shrugged, as if the conclusion was a no-brainer.

I smiled, reminding myself to have good manners. "Of course."

He studied me another minute before tilting his head. "You've really never played golf before?"

"Never." I had no shame in that admission.

He glanced back at the people mixing on the patio in the distance. At the little string quartet that played on the edge of the space. At the servers with trays in their hands as they moved in and out among people.

When he glanced back at me, he frowned. "Listen, why

don't you let me go teach you a few things? I'm not feeling very social right now anyway. I'd rather spend time with just you."

My throat tightened for no good reason. "Are we allowed to do that?"

"My father owns this course. So, yes. We are allowed to do this." His grin widened. "Come on. Just you and me. It will be fun."

After a moment of hesitation, I nodded. "Okay. But I have to tell you, I'm probably about as good at golf as I am at softball. Maybe, if I'm lucky, I'll make a slam dunk."

"Elle—" His face scrunched as he attempted to correct me.

"I'm just kidding," I quickly told him.

The confused look disappeared, followed by a chuckle.

"Of course you are." He nodded toward a golf cart that appeared to be waiting for us. "You ready to make that slam dunk?"

"Absolutely."

We climbed in, and Jono took off across the greens. A tremble of nerves rushed through me. I hoped I hadn't put myself in an awkward situation. But I had a feeling I had. I was good at doing that.

"I have to admit, I thought you were going to back out on me." Jono turned down a path leading to our first hole.

"Like I said, golf isn't really my thing." The answer was noncommittal—just as I'd planned.

He pushed on the brake, and the golf cart eased to a stop. He explained a few things to me about golf clubs—things I had no desire to learn—then he grabbed a couple from his bag, said something about normally using a caddy, and then climbed out. He motioned for me to follow as he took his place near what he called a tee box.

He gave me a few more instructions about swinging. I tried to listen. I really did.

My problem was that I didn't care. I tried hard not to show that.

As he lined up his shot, he said, "I have to admit, I'm not used to people telling me no."

He was still talking about the fact that I almost didn't come . . .

And the fact that people didn't usually tell him no didn't come as a surprise. "I . . . can imagine."

Jono swung his club and hit the golf ball. It flew across the greens. "So, I have to ask: Are you and Michael seeing each other?"

I felt heat rising up my neck when I realized I couldn't tell the entire truth right now. I hated lying. I hated it *so* much.

"We have a strange relationship," I finally said, strangling my golf club as I waited my turn. My nerves were getting the best of me. "But he needed some help with the softball team, so that's what I'm doing."

"Interesting."

I attempted to imitate Jono and line up a shot on the tee.

Apparently, I did it all wrong because Jono came over and wrapped his arms around me to show me how it should be done.

It was cliché, but Jono didn't seem to care. In fact, he seemed to enjoy it, to enjoy being close.

I had to admit that the man smelled good. Had I expected anything less from someone like Jono? Nope.

Despite his help as I swung, my ball landed far, far away from the hole in the distance. I wasn't surprised. That felt a bit like the investigation—I kept missing the mark.

"You'll get the hang of it." Jono waved his hand in the air like it wasn't a big deal. At least the man was gracious.

I used to think softball was the worst sport ever. But I've changed my mind. Golf was. What was so fun about chasing a little ball all over a course only to end up chasing it some more? When you made it a competition, it just seemed mind-numbing.

"I know this probably seems out of the blue, but you and Michael don't like each other very much, do you?" I asked him as we walked back toward the golf cart. I probably shouldn't have brought it up, but I just had so many questions that I wanted answers to—starting with that one.

Why I felt more comfortable asking Jono rather than Michael, I wasn't really sure. I'd have to examine that at another time.

He shrugged and studied my face a moment. "Michael didn't tell you?"

"Tell me what?" My heart pounded in my ears with expectation.

Jono pressed the accelerator, and we started toward his ball. "We were best friends in high school."

My eyes widened. I hadn't expected that. "What?"

"That's right. We did everything together. He was the preacher's kid, and I was the rich rebel. We were quite the duo."

I could only imagine. "What happened between the two of you?"

Jono's gaze darkened as he stared straight ahead. "Michael stole my girl."

I flinched, certain I hadn't heard him correctly. That did not fit with what I knew about Michael. "What?"

Jono shrugged. "I don't really like to talk about it. But there's definitely history between us. And we will never be friends again. Ever."

Michael was a girlfriend stealer? I just couldn't see it. But, based on Jono's body language, that was indeed what he thought happened.

Suddenly, it appeared I had one more mystery on my hands.

Just what I needed.

CHAPTER NINETEEN

FOUR HOLES LATER, Jono and I were still chasing those stupid balls.

I couldn't remember how much longer this golf lesson was going to last, but I had to make sure I didn't run out of time to ask questions before the session was complete—questions about his possible connection with my father.

As I lined up my shot, I tried to sound casual as I said, "I know you like to travel. Have you ever been to South America?"

I swung, and my ball flew across the greens. It landed in a sandpit.

Go figure.

"No, as a matter of fact, I haven't." He glanced at me as we walked across the greens. "Why do you ask?"

"It's just really beautiful there. I think everyone should

visit sometime. Of course, it helps if you know Spanish." I was fishing for more information, of course. A true Yerbian operative would know how to speak the language.

"I took a couple of years of it in high school. I can't say that I know that much, though. I know enough to say can you get me a drink." He let out a chuckle.

Instantly, I was filled with images of Jono sitting at a fancy resort and snapping his fingers to get the servers to bring him what he wanted when he wanted it.

I didn't like the pictures that formed in my head.

Maybe I really could rule Jono out. If he didn't speak Spanish and if he had never been to South America, then I had a hard time understanding how he could be involved with Yerba or my father.

So what had I heard him say that day?

I still had one more thing I wanted to talk to him about.

We climbed into the cart again.

As silence fell, I knew I had my opportunity. "It's really sad what happened to the coach, James Cruz, isn't it?"

"I know. Isn't that crazy? You just never know when your time is going to be up." He shrugged, his words seeming sincere instead of flippant.

"Some people are saying that maybe it wasn't an accident. What do you think?"

He blanched, his foot hitting the brake for just a second before he continued. "I don't see how it could be anything except an accident. But he did have enemies. However, if they were going to come after him, I would think there would be other ways."

"What do you mean by enemies?" Was I onto something?

He glanced at me and shrugged. "I'm probably not the best one to ask. But you should talk to his girlfriend, Tonya Birdsong. Maybe she has more information for you."

Two thoughts hit me. First, I saved Tonya Birdsong's name so I could look into her later.

My second thought was what exactly he'd just said. "Why did you say, 'maybe she has more information for you'?"

His head fell to the side, and he gave me a side glance. "You think I don't know that you and Michael are investigating something?"

"What?" It wasn't my most intelligent statement, but it was all I could think of to ask right now.

"You work for Driscoll and Associates. You and Michael are obviously coworkers. And you're obviously going undercover as boyfriend and girlfriend to investigate something."

So maybe Jono was a little smarter than I had given him credit for.

But that didn't matter right now. What mattered was that I had found out that James had a girlfriend. Michael and I definitely needed to talk to her ASAP.

As he walked toward the golf cart, he sang a song to himself. "Mañana, Alexa . . ."

I froze.

What?

And the cadence of the words almost made it sound like he was saying *mantente alerta*.

The phrase my father had said.

But Jono wasn't saying that at all.

He was singing a silly song.

I'd been off track this whole time, hadn't I? I shook my head. How could I have been so wrong?

***

THAT NIGHT, my phone rang, startling me out of my sleep.

I glanced at the time on the clock beside my bed. 1:30 a.m. Who could be calling at this hour?

But when I looked at my screen, I saw Michael's number and quickly answered.

"What's going on? Is everything okay?" Thinking the worst wasn't my normal MO. But, in times like this, it felt appropriate. Too many people with blood in their eyes were close.

"Elliot?"

It wasn't Michael's voice I heard on the other end. No, it was his daughter, Chloe's.

My alarm grew even more. "Chloe? This is Elliot. Are you okay?"

"My grandparents are out of town," she said, her voice just above a whisper. "And my dad is sick. I don't know what to do."

I sat up, my blanket falling at my waist. "What do you mean sick?"

"He's lying on the couch, and he's moaning. Plus, he feels hot. Like lava. Should I call 911?" Her voice cracked, and I could tell the girl was scared for her father's sake.

"You stay where you are. I will be over to your place in ten minutes, okay?"

"Okay. But I'm scared. Is my dad going to be okay?"

"He's going to be fine. Just hold tight until I get there, okay?"

"Come fast, Elliot. Please."

As I ended the call, I tried to resist the surge of panic that wanted to rush through me. This was no time to be irrational. I needed to think clearly if I was going to help Michael out.

He'd said earlier today he'd felt like he had some allergies coming on or something. Maybe it wasn't an allergy at all but a virus.

I quickly threw some clothes on and grabbed my purse. I left a note for my mom, so she wouldn't get worried. And then I was out the door.

CHAPTER TWENTY

I FOUND Michael's address online, and I rushed to get there.

I'd never been to his house before. I felt a little weird to be going like this the first time, but an emergency was an emergency. Still, part of me was curious to see where he lived.

As I drove, the dark road stared behind me. Familiar goosebumps scattered across my skin again.

There was no one else out here on the stretch of asphalt. So why did I feel like I was being watched?

I had no idea.

I gripped my steering wheel more tightly.

I couldn't wait to get to Michael's place. Being alone always made me feel more vulnerable. When I considered the fact that unseen enemies from Yerba could be after me, as well as the Beltway Killer, I was on edge—and rightfully so.

Ten minutes later, I pulled up to a large estate, and I pressed on my brake.

I looked at the address on my phone again.

The two matched.

This was not what I had expected. No, the three-story brick house was probably located on two acres of land.

Then again, that large house was probably his parents'. They were pastors at a mega church in the area, and I had the impression that money was not a problem for them. I wrestled with the reality of that—but this wasn't the time to dwell on it.

But just beyond that house, I saw lights glowing in the window of a second structure in the back.

I was going to have to guess that's where Michael and Chloe lived.

I released my foot from the brake and kept heading down the driveway toward the light. As soon as I put my car into Park, I saw the front door open and Chloe stepped out.

Just as I expected, there were tears in her eyes.

This had shaken her up.

I rushed toward her and put my hands on her arms, trying to calm her down. "Where is your dad?"

"He's on the couch."

"Take me to him."

Chloe took my hand and led me through the foyer, past a formal dining area, and into a den at the back of the house.

I saw a figure lying on the couch there with a blanket. Soft moans escaped from him.

I rushed to Michael's side and examined him.

A sheen of sweat had spread across his forehead. Even in the darkness, he somehow seemed pale. And he definitely wasn't lucid. Chloe had been running around and a visitor had come into his house and he hadn't even noticed.

That was not like protective Michael.

"Do you have a thermometer?" I asked Chloe as I knelt on the floor.

She nodded beside me. "I think."

"Go see if you can find it for me. Please."

As she scrambled away, I put my hand to Michael's forehead. It was just like Chloe had said. He was burning up.

I went into the kitchen and found a paper towel. I wet it and squeezed the excess water out. Then I went back to Michael and rested it on his forehead. He let out another little moan and jerked.

My heart pounded into my rib cage. I'd never seen Michael like this before. He was always so in control. But not now.

Chloe came back with a thermometer, and I took his temperature. One hundred three degrees.

That was high for an adult, but not so incredibly high

that we needed to call 911. I would need to monitor him. If his fever went up any, then I would seek backup.

"Can you do me another favor?" I asked Chloe. "Can you get me a bottle of water and some Tylenol? Do you know what that looks like?"

She nodded. "I do."

"Great. Go bring those things back to me."

She scrambled away again. I figured it was better for her to keep her thoughts occupied.

When she returned, I realized I needed to figure out how to get Michael to take this medicine in his current state. Carefully, I nudged his shoulders up. I sat behind him, my body acting as a prop for his head and shoulders.

Then I took two of the Tylenol from the bottle and held them in my palm. I unscrewed the bottle of water so it would be ready. Then I braced myself for my next challenge.

"Michael, can you hear me?" I shook him, needing him to be halfway lucid, at least.

He moaned.

"Michael? I need you to take this medicine for me."

He moaned again.

He certainly wasn't going to make this easy for me, was he?

"Michael," I repeated.

I shook him harder this time. His eyes barely opened, and he let out something that almost sounded like a "huh."

"I need you to take these." I held up the pills.

Somehow, he managed to grab them from me and slip them into his mouth. He grabbed the water and chugged it. Then his eyes closed again.

As they did, his body seemed to collapse, with me beneath it.

Almost instantly, he seemed dead to the world.

Chloe glanced at me, questions floating in her gaze.

"He's going to be okay," I whispered. "He needs to get some rest."

"Are you leaving?" Her voice quivered.

"I'm going to stay with him until I know he's okay," I said, knowing I couldn't let Chloe handle this alone. "But you have school tomorrow, don't you?"

She nodded.

"Why don't you go to bed, and I'll stay out here with your dad and keep an eye on him. Is that okay?"

She nodded, but still looked uncertain.

"It's fine," I assured her. "I promise that I will take good care of him."

"Thank you, Elliot . . ."

"You're welcome."

With one more glance at her dad, she stepped closer and kissed his forehead. "I love you, Daddy."

The next instant she started back toward the hallway but stopped. "I don't want to go back there by myself."

I glanced at the loveseat beside the couch. "Why don't

you grab that blanket from the back of the couch and see if you can sleep on that loveseat instead?"

She nodded, almost as if relieved. The next instant, she grabbed a blanket and pillow, and she cuddled on the couch.

A few minutes later, everything went still in the house.

I glanced at Michael as his head rested in my lap. I wasn't sure what he was going to think about this when he became lucid again. Maybe once I was sure he was sleeping well, I would try to somehow slip from beneath him.

As I sat there, I remembered Jono's words. Had Michael really stolen his friend's girlfriend? I had trouble seeing him as the type. Would that change how I viewed him if it was true?

I wasn't sure.

We all made mistakes when we were younger. And I knew that Michael's past had included a rebellious streak where he'd walked away from everything he'd been raised to believe.

Still, the idea of it bothered me more than I thought it would.

But for now, I put my head back onto the couch and closed my eyes. I placed my hand on his forehead, telling myself it was so I could monitor his fever. His silky hair rested beneath my fingers.

Funny that I had never thought about touching his hair before. But now that I was, I liked the feel of it. My other hand rested against his arm, allowing me to feel the thick muscles there also.

This was no time to be thinking about those things.

I was just thankful that Chloe trusted me enough to call me when she needed me.

Maybe I could get a little shuteye like this until Michael woke up. I functioned so much better with sleep, after all.

But I was having trouble getting comfortable enough to actually fall asleep.

As I felt Michael shift on my lap, I pulled my eyes open.

Michael was staring at me. Except his eyes looked glazed and not quite with it.

"Elliot?" Michael stared at me.

I tried to offer a reassuring smile. "It's me."

He grabbed my hand and nestled it against his chest. "I'm glad you're here."

"I'm glad I can help too. I kept my voice low so I wouldn't wake Chloe.

"Oh, Elliot . . ." His eyes bore into mine.

Something about the way he said my name made my heart skip a beat.

"I know I've never told you this," he said, his voice sounding raspy. "But I love you."

My heart pounded in my ears. Certainly, I hadn't heard him correctly. Or he was delirious. Or both.

As if to confirm my suspicions, Michael's eyes closed again and he fell into a sound slumber.

I was going to write those words off as an accident, something said under the influence of the fever. Certainly, he hadn't meant it.

But, if that was true, then why did disappointment stretch through me?

CHAPTER TWENTY-ONE

I STARTLED AWAKE the next morning.

Glanced around.

Realized I had no idea where I was.

Then I looked down and saw Michael's head resting in my lap, and everything flooded back to me.

The phone call from Chloe. Michael's fever. The words that Michael had muttered.

I love you.

Now that it was morning, I was more certain than ever that Michael had just said that while in a state of delirium. But that didn't change me from feeling a touch of delight and then disappointment at knowing his statement wasn't true.

Neither of those emotions were ones that I had expected.

As I shifted, Michael's eyes flew open. I rested my hand against his cheek, trying to figure out if his fever had broken.

He felt much cooler now than he had last night. That was something to be thankful for.

He groaned and pushed himself up. "Elliot?"

That's what I thought. He probably didn't remember anything, did he? Maybe it was better that way.

Before he could say anything, Chloe stirred. She sprang from the loveseat and bounced over to her dad.

"Daddy! Daddy! Daddy. Are you okay? I was so worried."

Michael rubbed his head as if confused. "I'm fine. What happened?"

"Your fever spiked last night, and it made Chloe nervous. She called me to come over to make sure you were okay."

Michael's eyebrows flickered up before he glanced at Chloe. "Is that right? You didn't have to call Elliot, sweetheart."

"No," I said. "It's totally fine that she did. She was worried, and I'm glad that I could be here for her."

"Wow." He blinked several times. "I must have really been out of it, huh?"

"You were. Your fever was up to 103. If it climbed any higher, I was going to take you to the ER." I studied his face, trying to get a read on how he was this morning. "How are you?"

"I feel . . . okay, I guess. A little sluggish, but I don't feel achy anymore."

"Your fever could still spike again," I said. "You should keep an eye on it, just to be safe."

"I'm sure I'll be fine."

I stood, realizing I should probably get going. "You should stay home today and take care of yourself. I can handle things with the investigation."

"We have practice tonight . . ."

"I can handle it." As soon as the words left my lips, I wondered what in the world I was talking about. I was in no way, shape, or form ready to handle practice. But I also knew that Michael couldn't handle it today either.

"Elliot—"

"No, I mean it. You need to take care of yourself. Besides, nobody wants your germs right now."

"She's right, Daddy." Chloe sat beside her dad and put her arm around him. "I would stay home and take care of you, but I have to get ready for school. Do you want me to miss school? Because I will if you need me."

A faint smile crossed his lips. "No, sweetheart. I'll be just fine. Thank you. Why don't you run off and get ready for school? I'm going to tell Elliot goodbye."

"Okay, Daddy." She scampered off down the hallway.

As she did, Michael rose to his feet and turned toward me, a certain vulnerability in his eyes that I hadn't seen before. "Thanks for coming over, Elliot. I'm sorry you had to go to all this trouble."

"Like I said, it's really no problem. I'm glad I could be there to make Chloe feel better, at least."

He shifted and rubbed his jaw. "I didn't . . . say anything weird, did I?"

I swallowed hard as I remembered his words. After a moment of contemplation, I finally shook my head. "No, you were fine. Just feverish. Maybe you drooled a little."

He chuckled, and something that looked close to relief washed through his gaze. "Okay. Good. But I really do want to go to work—"

"And I really don't think you should," I said, my voice sounding more decisive than usual. "When do you think you started feeling feverish?"

"I guess it was about three o'clock or something."

"Then you at least need to wait until twenty-four hours have passed with no fever." It was probably supposed to be longer than that, but I was trying to be gracious.

He frowned and fell back against the couch. "Fine. But only because I'm trying to set a good example for Chloe."

"I'll check in with you if I need anything, okay?"

"You promise?"

"I do." Then I punched his arm and tried to forget his feverish confession. "Now you take care of yourself."

***

"WHERE'S MICHAEL?" Velma asked when I walked into the office.

I'd taken just enough time to go home, eat breakfast, and

shower before coming into the office. But I was ten minutes late.

Michael was always right on time.

I had no idea why Velma might think I knew where he was.

"He's not feeling well," I said. "I told him he should stay home and recuperate."

Curiosity darted through Velma's gaze. "I see. I hope he feels better."

"Me too. In the meantime, I guess I'm on my own today." I took a sip of my coffee. I was going to need some extra caffeine today.

"You want company?" Velma asked.

I paused near my office. "You want to help me?"

She shrugged. "Sometimes I like to get out there and do fieldwork. Besides, Oscar isn't coming in today either. He decided he wanted to play golf. I was going to go dumpster diving in the unit behind the office, but I'm not feeling it today."

"I see."

I couldn't think of any good excuse for Velma not to go with me. Besides, if she went dumpster diving, she'd probably end up finding some discarded food from the bakery two doors down and offer it to me.

"Sure thing," I finally said. "If you're game, so am I."

A bright smile flashed across her face.

"Great." She plucked up her purse and stood. "I'm ready

when you are."

Twenty minutes later, I was heading out with Velma to track down James Cruz's girlfriend, Tonya Birdsong.

"So, you talked to Michael this morning?" Velma asked, pulling a roll of toilet paper from her purse. As I drove, she began splitting the two-ply.

I didn't ask.

"I did. His daughter got nervous last night when he was sick and she called me." That seemed like the simplest enough explanation and shouldn't raise any eyebrows.

"Oh."

It may have only been one word, but it was loaded.

"I'm glad to see Michael has finally found a sidekick who's decent," Velma said.

I glanced at her as I came to a stop sign. "Do you mean the ones before me at Driscoll and Associates weren't?"

"Some of them may have been smart enough, but they were irritating. One guy liked to pick his toes all the time. One girl apparently had a crush on Michael. Another one was writing a mystery novel and thought she could get some firsthand experience. As you probably know, most of them lasted only a week or two at the most. You're setting a new record."

Well, I could be thankful for that.

"And I know it doesn't seem like Oscar likes you, but Oscar is a very hard guy to please." Velma studied her cherry-colored fingernails. "I really think that he does like you."

"I thought you and Michael were the only ones he liked."

"Michael and I both have histories with Oscar," Velma said.

My interest perked. "Do you?"

"Oscar helped me out of a tight spot with my ex-husband. The man was abusive, and I had no money. Oscar stepped in and took my case when nobody else would."

"I didn't think he did pro bono cases." Oscar and I had a big argument over that not long ago.

"He doesn't. And that's why I work for him now."

"I see." I swallowed hard, contemplating whether or not I should ask the next question. "And Michael has a story like that too?"

"You mean he's never told you?" Surprise laced Velma's voice.

I shook my head.

"Oh, yes. Michael has a story too. But I'll let him tell you sometime. I'd hate to spoil the fun."

And that was the way that it should be. I knew that. But that didn't stop me from feeling disappointed.

It was just as well.

I pulled up to the house of Tonya Birdsong. I hoped that maybe she would have some answers concerning her boyfriend's death.

CHAPTER TWENTY-TWO

TONYA BIRDSONG WAS everything I had imagined her to be. She was probably in her early twenties, with dark hair that had been pulled back into a perfect ponytail. She had defined arms, a bounce in her step, and her athleisure outfit confirmed she was a fitness addict.

She seemed just the kind of person that someone like James Cruz would like.

When Velma and I had arrived, she didn't shoo us away—surprisingly. Instead, we sat in the living room of a moderately sized home in a suburb of Storm River.

"How did you know about me and James?" She took a long sip of some type of chocolate protein shake and eyed us.

"Somebody mentioned it yesterday at the golf tournament," I said.

She let out a little grunt. "James wanted to keep our relationship quiet."

"Why is that?" I wasn't judging her. I had been engaged, and I had kept much of that relationship a secret also. It was partly because I was engaged to my boss, and it was also partly because my family didn't like him.

I should have listened to my mom and dad because it turned out Sergio was working for the very regime that had overthrown the government in Yerba.

But that was a story for a different day.

"James said it helped his reputation as a consultant if people thought he was single." Tonya scowled before taking another long sip of her protein shake. She sat perched on a bar stool near the island that separated the kitchen from the living room.

Translation: if he could flirt, James got better results at his job.

"How did that make you feel?" Velma asked.

I wasn't sure, but she appeared to be eyeballing some plastic cups on top of the trashcan.

I'd bet anything she wanted to snag them, wash them, and reuse them.

I couldn't let her do that.

Tonya shrugged. "At first, I didn't like it. But I suppose that made sense."

"How long did you guys date?" I watched her expression, trying to pick up on any subtle nuances.

"Only about six months. And then we broke up." She said it almost half-heartedly, like she didn't really care.

"Wait." I shifted on the couch. "So you weren't still dating?"

"We were up until three days before he died in the car accident." Tonya's voice cracked, and she looked away, moisture filling her gaze.

She obviously still had feelings for the man. It made sense. Her nonchalant façade was just that—a façade.

"What happened?" Velma pulled her gaze away from the trashcan. "Why did you break up?"

"I found out he was seeing somebody else behind my back." Tonya pushed her lips together, and her neck tightened. She definitely cared more than she wanted to admit. She'd really liked Cruz, hadn't she?

Wasn't that an interesting discovery? "Do you know who he was seeing?"

"No, I don't. But, about a week ago, I picked up his phone when he went to the bathroom. A text popped up—a text that made it very clear he was seeing someone else."

"Did you confront him?" I tried to picture how it all played out.

"James denied it. He said he didn't know where the text came from. Isn't that the most ridiculous thing that you've ever heard?" Tonya rolled her eyes.

"He gave no indications who it might be from?" I asked.

"No, but I have a feeling it was with somebody on that stupid softball team."

"Why do you think that?" I asked.

"Because the text had weird baseball terminology—it said, 'Let's score a home run tonight' followed by a kissing emoji. I hoped James and I might have more time to talk about it. But, obviously, that didn't happen."

I leaned toward her. "Do you think his death was an accident?"

She rubbed her throat, as if fighting emotions still. "I've heard some people don't. James could be a hothead at times. But I don't think it's out of the realm of possibility that it was truly an accident."

"Do you have any idea where he was heading that night?" I continued.

"No, but I do know that he had not been acting like himself the week or two before he died. He always seemed like he was sweating and looking at his phone."

"Did you ever ask him about it?"

"I did," Tonya said. "He said it was nothing to worry over. That he had found some type of new financial opportunity he wanted to explore."

I glanced at Velma. The same understanding that usually passed between Michael and I did not pass between the two of us. But certainly Velma understood that we may have finally found a lead—unless she was still thinking about those Solo cups. That was a real possibility.

If Cruz really was murdered, then maybe it had something to do with either this new girlfriend or this new opportunity.

AS WE WALKED BACK to my car, several thoughts went through my mind.

But the predominant one was a memory of that first day of practice. Of when Mischa Harrington had been beside that tribute wall with tears in her eyes.

Was she the mystery woman that Tonya had mentioned?

It was my best guess. I knew whom I needed to talk to next. I just had to figure out a way of doing it without making her suspicious. It wasn't like the woman worked, so I couldn't stop by her place of business. That probably meant I was going to need to wait until practice tonight. A surprising rush of impatience fluttered through me.

Velma paused by some trash that had been left at the curbside.

Other people didn't embarrass me easily, but having my companion go through someone's trashcan almost made me cringe. It was hard to look professional while going through someone's garbage.

"Velma . . ." I pleaded with her to leave it alone.

"This is a really nice leather portfolio." Velma held it up. "I can't believe she would throw this away."

"We should go."

She shoved it under her arm. "Sure thing."

"So what do you think?" Velma asked as we climbed into my car.

"Definitely some interesting revelations," I said as I cranked my engine.

Or should I say as I *tried* to crank my engine. It took a few attempts before it finally roared to life. I guess that's what I got for driving a clunker. But it was happening more and more often recently. I hoped I could wait until after my sister's surgery to buy a new vehicle.

"So what next?" Velma asked as we sat there for a moment.

What were we going to do next? What would Michael say if he was here with me?

I glanced at the time. I should officially have a break before softball tonight. And I was going to need some time to get my thoughts together before I had to run practice. I needed to do some research so I didn't majorly mess up when talking to the team.

Plus, I still couldn't stop thinking about Grayson. I desperately wanted an update on what was going on with him. But I had promised Michael that I wouldn't look into his disappearance alone. With everything that was going on, that was becoming harder and harder.

"I think for now we need to go back to the office for a little bit," I finally said. "I need to get some stuff together for tonight's practice. I'm not going to talk to any of the women on the team until I get there this evening."

"That's probably a good idea. Speaking of which, how many women are on the team?"

"Only three. So, if James was dating someone, it should be easy to narrow down who. Plus, one of the women is in her fifties. She seems happily married, so I doubt it was her. That just leaves Mischa and Reni."

Before I put the car in Drive, my phone buzzed. I looked down at the screen and saw that Hunter had texted me.

As soon as I saw his name, my heart pounded with familiar guilt.

Why did I always feel guilty? It was my go-to emotion, it seemed. It didn't even matter if I logically knew I shouldn't feel guilty. For some reason, I still did.

Hunter and I weren't even officially dating. We were just getting to know each other. And Michael may have told me that he loved me, but he had been delirious and he didn't remember it.

His words were meaningless. Nothing was going to change between Michael and me.

But, despite all of that reasoning, my head still felt like it was spinning. And that wasn't even to mention anything about my heart.

I glanced down at the screen and read Hunter's words.

I appreciate you sharing your feelings, but I really need to take things slowly. I'm sorry.

I flinched as I read the words. What in the world was Hunter talking about?

I hadn't shared my feelings. What had made him think I had?

A bad feeling brewed in my gut.

CHAPTER TWENTY-THREE

I TYPED BACK: **What do you mean?**

A moment later, Hunter replied.

The text you sent this morning.

I hadn't texted Hunter this morning, so I had no idea what he was talking about.

I typed: **Are you sure you didn't get it mixed up with someone else?**

A moment later, a screenshot appeared on my phone. My eyes widened as I studied it. By all accounts, it definitely appeared I'd sent Hunter a text expressing just how much he meant to me.

I glanced at the time on the screenshot: 10:18. I had been talking to Tonya. I definitely hadn't sent that text while I was at her house.

Quickly, I typed back: **I don't know what's going on, but I did not send you that text. I don't know what else to say.**

When he didn't instantly type back, I did.

Awkward silence. Chirp. Chirp.

He still didn't respond. Great. This was as uncomfortable as wearing a quail costume to the Festival of the Chicken.

"What's going on?" Velma asked, glancing over my shoulder as we sat in front of Tonya's place.

"Hunter claims I texted him today spilling my guts about how much I liked him," I said. "Not only did I not say those things, but I couldn't have. That text was sent while we were talking to Tonya."

Velma's eyebrows furrowed. "That's weird."

I nibbled on my bottom lip a moment. "Is it possible that somebody could have sent a text from my number without me knowing?"

I felt crazy even asking that question.

Velma shrugged. "Maybe."

I leaned back in my seat and let that sink in. I didn't like the conclusions my mind wanted to draw.

Because if that was the case, what if somebody had sent those texts on Coach Cruz's phone also? What if he had somehow been set up? That could change this whole case.

I needed to really think that through and do some research before I shared the theory with anyone.

"Look at this," Velma muttered. She held up a piece of

paper in her hand, one that she'd plucked from the leather portfolio.

"What is it?"

"It's a receipt to a casino up in Jersey," she said. "James Cruz's name is on it, and it's dated two weeks ago."

"You think James had a gambling problem?" I asked.

She nodded. "I think it's a good possibility."

"Anything else in there?"

"I'll keep looking."

I put my car in Drive and headed back to the office. As soon as we got back and I sat down at my desk, Michael called. I had a lot to talk to him about.

"How are you feeling?" I asked, remembering his proclamation from last night. I quickly put it out of my mind. There was no need to dwell on that now.

"I'm feeling better. It must have just been a twenty-four-hour thing. Less than twenty-four hours, really."

"I'm glad." I glanced at my watch and saw it was just past lunchtime. "You should still take it easy."

"I suppose. How did things go this morning?"

I filled him in about my meeting with Tonya.

"Good job. Are you going to talk to Mischa and Reni tonight?"

"I'm going to try to casually bring it up and see if I can figure out which of them may have been seen with their previous coach before he died."

"Good job. Just try not to do that when you're with them alone. Try to make sure there are plenty of people around."

"Will do."

"One other thing I need to mention." Michael's voice sounded perky, like he really was feeling better. That was good news.

"I just got a call from the newspaper." He explained that a reporter was coming out to do a story on the upcoming game. Michael had already talked to a few of the players who would be interviewed.

"Are they going to interview me?" A small flash of terror pummeled me at the thought.

"I'm not sure. I would try to avoid that if I were you. Especially since you haven't mastered all the correct baseball terminology yet."

"Yeah, probably a good idea." I frowned as I imagined the mistakes that might come out of my mouth. "One more thing."

"What's up?" Michael asked.

I swallowed hard, dreading what I had to say. "Hunter got a text from me today, a text that I didn't send him."

"Okay . . ."

"I've been researching if it's possible for someone to hijack your phone number and send texts to people—texts that appear to come from you. It is possible."

"What are you getting at, Elliot?"

"That text Cruz sent right before his accident . . . what if he didn't actually send it? What if someone sent it to make him look irresponsible?"

Michael let out a grunt. "There's a theory. You could be onto something. But why would someone send a fake text from you also?"

"Maybe we're closer to finding answers than we thought."

"You could be right," Michael said. "If you learn anything else, let me know. Otherwise, good luck tonight. And be careful."

"I'll probably need all the luck I can get."

"Knock 'em dead, Elliot."

Knock them dead? I wasn't sure exactly what that meant, but it didn't sound good.

THE REPORTER SHOWED up at the baseball field right before we started practice. Her name was Kitty Kight, and she was around my age. She had curly blonde hair that fell to her shoulders and a bright smile, along with a smattering of freckles.

I introduced her to the players she was supposed to interview. As she got quotes from them, I carefully watched everyone around me, looking for any sign of guilt.

I didn't see anything suspicious.

What if all of this was for nothing? I mean, I suppose it wouldn't be *nothing* nothing. Michael and I were still getting paid to investigate. But sometimes I had to wonder if Cruz's accident was truly just an accident.

I really missed having Michael here to help me navigate the next step. But I was going to have to be a big girl right now and do this myself. As long as I was careful, I should be fine.

After Kitty interviewed the last player, she approached me near my spot in the dugout. "I hear you're the assistant coach. Can I get a quote from you?"

"I prefer you give their real coach a call and get a quote from him," I told her. "I can't say this is really something I'm an expert on."

"You could at least tell me if you think it's important that the food bank is getting a donation."

"Well, of course. People shouldn't have to go hungry, so the cause behind this ballgame is a very worthy one. I do hope the community will come out and help support the nonprofit by watching the game. Bring some canned food and bring yourself. It's going to be a good time."

Kitty smiled and lowered her recorder. "Perfect. You're new in town, right?"

"I am."

"I figured I would have seen you around before. How do you like it here in Storm River?"

How did I answer that honestly?

"It's certainly a unique place." Maybe I should go into

politics. I was pretty good at giving lukewarm answers when I had to.

"Well, I think it's great that you've jumped in and gotten involved with the community." Kitty put her recorder away and nodded. "I'll let you get to practice. I might stand in the background and take a few pictures. Is that okay?"

How wrong could we go with pictures? As long as I wasn't in any of them, it should be fine. And I didn't plan on being on the field so we should all be good.

Right?

CHAPTER TWENTY-FOUR

I WAS DELIGHTED when Mischa Harrington had arrived early to practice. She was just the person I wanted to talk to.

She glanced at me with uncertainty in her eyes as she set her bag in the dugout.

"Where is Michael?" she asked with what almost sounded like trepidation in her voice.

"He's not feeling well, so I'm taking over practice tonight."

Mischa's eyes widened, and I saw the doubt there—doubt that I could handle something like this. I couldn't deny that I felt a good measure of that myself.

"I was hoping I might be able to grab a few minutes with you," I started, gripping my clipboard.

Her doubt turned into caution, and she took a step back. "What's going on?"

"I know about you and Coach Cruz." I decided to start with that assumption and see how she reacted.

Her eyes widened even more. "What . . . what do you mean?"

"The two of you were seeing each other."

Her cheeks looked flushed. "We'd only gone out a few times. It wasn't a big deal."

At least she didn't deny it. "Did you know that he had a girlfriend?"

"He told me they broke up." She raised her chin defiantly. "But I suspect they weren't broken up when we went out the first time."

"That's the only reason you're playing in this game, isn't it? You're just about as good at it as I am. I should have realized that earlier."

She shrugged. "I've had a 'crush' on the man for a long time. What can I say? It's hard being a single lady sometimes. But if you think I killed him, you're wrong."

As her surprise wore off, her snootiness kicked in.

"Do you know where he was going that night?" I continued, gripping a softball in my hands.

"He had gotten a text from somebody he wanted to meet about selling his car."

I paused, wondering if I had heard her correctly. "He was selling his car? I heard he loved that car."

Mischa shrugged again. "That's right. I'm not sure what was going on with James, but he seemed like he wanted to get his hands on some more cash."

Like most of the people in this town.

"Speaking of selling his car, did he ever say anything to you about selling his house?" I asked.

She shook her head and grabbed a bat from her bag. She gripped it in her hands, practicing her swing.

I tried not to think about how it would feel if that sporting equipment were to hit me.

I swallowed hard, hoping I never had to find out.

"Like I said, we had only seen each other a few times," Mischa finally said, still warming up her swing. "Not really enough to talk about things like that in depth."

"I heard he had a gambling problem."

Mischa scrunched her face before shaking her head. "No, he absolutely didn't. But he did mention to me that he discovered someone he knew had a gambling problem. He wanted to get him help. I'm pretty sure he borrowed money from my dad to help pay off this person's debt."

"Why would you say that?"

"Just some conversations that I overheard. Nothing I can prove. And my dad won't ever talk about money stuff. He's tight-lipped when it comes to that. Always has been."

I stored that information away. "Last question. I promise. Do you know if Cruz had enemies?"

Her face went a little paler, and she shrugged. "I don't really know. But if I had to guess? Coach Beasley."

That was an interesting response. "Why exactly would you say that?"

"Because Beasley is one of these guys who wants to win whatever the cost." Her voice hardened as she said the words. She obviously didn't appreciate the man's attitude.

"You think Beasley would kill in order to do that?" It seemed outlandish to me. Then again, maybe wealth, politics, social status, and sports all went hand in hand in this area.

Mischa paused from swinging the bat and let out a long sigh. "I don't know. I wish I did. I just know . . . Beasley goes overboard sometimes. I heard he was trying to put everyone on his team on a special high-protein diet. He has them do a lot more drills and even makes them practice more."

I studied her face for another moment, something clicking in my mind. "You're the one who called in the anonymous tip, aren't you? The one who said she saw Coach Beasley messing with Cruz's car?"

She rubbed her throat and glanced around, as if to make sure no one else was listening. "That was me. I want to catch whoever did this just as bad as anybody. I've been on edge ever since I learned what happened. James wasn't a saint, but he didn't deserve to be murdered—if that's what happened."

At least we were on the same page there. "If you hear anything, will you let me know?"

She nodded and took a step back. "Of course."

As more people arrived, I knew our conversation was over. Now I had to face my next challenge.

I had to somehow get through this practice while keeping my sanity.

AFTER PRACTICE, I looked over and saw Michael and Chloe sitting in the stands watching.

My stomach sank.

Great. Michael had seen all of that, hadn't he? And, by all of that, I meant when I'd used the wrong terminology, when I'd started to run toward third base instead of first, and when the pitching machine mysteriously started going off and a ball had hit me in the back.

Not my finest moments.

I'd had no choice but to be on the field and participate, however.

I slowly walked toward them and tried to plaster on my best smile. "Wasn't expecting to see you guys here."

Chloe sprang off the bench and ran over to me, throwing her arms around my legs. "Elliot! Elliot! I'm so glad to see you."

At once, some of my self-consciousness disappeared.

"It's really good to see you too, Chloe." I glanced back at Michael. "I guess you're feeling better."

He nodded. "Like nothing ever happened. Must have been some type of twelve-hour virus or something."

"I'm glad you could make it." I tried not to grit my teeth as I said the words. The last thing I wanted was for someone to see me fail, which was precisely what had happened tonight. I'd been doing a lot of mental rhyming. Like a *lot* a lot.

"That was a really good catch that you tried to make." His lips twitched as if he was trying hard not to smile.

I narrowed my eyes. "I was trying my best."

"I thought you did great, Elliot." Chloe smiled up at me.

I hugged Chloe again before giving Michael a pointed look. "Thank you, sweetie."

"I figured I could at least help you clean up a little bit around here." Michael rose from the stands and met me, waving hello to several players as they left and exchanging a few words of conversation with them.

Afterward, he helped me gather the practice balls and bases.

"How did the interviews go?" Michael asked as we met back at the stands.

"Okay, I guess. The reporter seemed nice enough."

"Never trust a nice reporter." Michael leaned against the bleachers.

I grabbed the clipboard and gave him a look. "For real?"

"It's always the nice reporters who take you out of left field."

"Is that literal or figurative?"

"Figurative. The snakelike reporters? You can spot them a mile away and know you need to be cautious. It's the nice ones who catch you by surprise."

"I'll keep that in mind."

"Elliot, come back to our house," Chloe said. "We're having banana splits. She can come too, can't she, Dad?"

"I'm sure she has other things to do." Michael shifted, almost as if he felt awkward.

"Please, Dad! We owe her." Chloe gave her dad her best puppy dog eyes.

"I don't want to impose," I said, trying to politely decline.

"You wouldn't be imposing. Right, Daddy?"

Michael shrugged and shoved his hands into his jeans pockets. "If Elliot would like to come, then we would love to have her."

I gave him a look, trying to read his expression. "Really?"

"Really." He shrugged again but his gaze remained on me, no regret in his eyes.

"Okay then," I said. "I would love to experience my first banana split with the two of you. Believe it or not, I've never had one. But, just last week, my sister was talking about them."

Michael's eyebrows shot up. "Your first, huh?"

"That's right. As far as I know, they don't exist in Yerba."

"You're going to be in love," Michael said.

I swallowed hard when he used the word "love." All I knew was that some time away from this case and everything that was happening sounded refreshing. Maybe it would be just what my mind needed.

"Let's find out if these banana splits live up to their hype or not," I said.

"Oh, they will, Elliot." Chloe nodded. "They will."

CHAPTER TWENTY-FIVE

THIRTY MINUTES LATER, we were at Michael's place. Since these circumstances were different than those of last night, I had a better chance to check out his humble abode.

Michael and Chloe lived in a small cottage behind Michael's parents' three-story, all brick estate. The place was stately with a well-manicured lawn and flowerbeds. Really, the whole property was lovely.

I thought it was nice that Michael could be so close to his parents. Plus, I knew they were a huge help since Michael was a single dad. His place was fairly well decorated. If I had to guess, his mom had helped.

"So, what do you think, Elliot?" Chloe put a bite of chocolate-covered, sprinkle-laced ice cream into her mouth as soon as she asked the question.

"I'm pretty sure God designed these flavors to go together," I told her, holding up a spoonful of my own banana split. "I just might need a few more sprinkles."

She grinned from across the kitchen table. "Sprinkles make everything better, don't they?"

"I'm inclined to agree." I picked up the bottle full of the colorful confections and added more to the top of my ice cream creation.

"You two were made for each other." Michael shook his head and added a spray of whipped cream to his dessert. "Something about the texture of sprinkles just messes up the whole experience."

"No, you're totally wrong."

Chloe grinned, some of the chocolate syrup clinging to the edges of her lips. "Yeah, Dad. Totally wrong."

He smiled and shook his head. "I can see that I'm outnumbered, so I'll keep my mouth shut for now. A mouth that is absent of any sprinkles I might add."

"That just means more for us," I told Chloe.

She giggled.

I had to admit that this was a nice detour. Really nice, and quite surprising. It wasn't exactly the way I'd seen my day going, but I wasn't complaining.

The three of us continued to eat and chitchat. For a moment, I almost forgot about all my problems—and I had a lot of them to forget about.

A few minutes later, Michael's phone buzzed. He looked at the screen and frowned.

I waited, hoping it was an update and assuming it was something about the case. But I really had no idea.

Michael finally put his phone back into his pocket. "That was my friend, the mechanic."

I lowered my spoon and waited for him to continue. "And?"

"And . . . he didn't see anything wrong with Cruz's car. Based on the report that we showed him, it doesn't appear that the brake line was cut or that anything else went wrong."

I blanched in surprise. "Really?"

That hadn't been what I had expected to hear. Not by a long shot.

"I'm not sure whether or not I should say that is good news or bad news," I muttered.

"Same here." Michael frowned and shoved his spoon into a mound of vanilla ice cream.

I knew he was thinking the same thing I was. Cruz's death may not be a case at all. There was no evidence that this was murder. James Cruz may have died simply because of a moment of carelessness behind the wheel.

And if that was the case, where did that leave our investigation? The only thing that gave me any hope was that fake text message that had been sent to Hunter from my number.

But did that really prove anything?

I wasn't sure.

AN HOUR LATER, I was still at Michael's house. We had played board games, laughed some more, and generally had a good time. Chloe had shown me her room and talked me into braiding her hair.

As I secured the end with a little band, I caught a glance of Chloe watching me in the mirror.

"Most girls my age have moms," she said.

My heart slowed for a beat as I heard some of the pain in her words. "Does that bother you?"

"Not most of the time. But one day she's going to come back."

Where had she gotten that idea? "Oh, is that what your dad says?"

She shrugged. "No. But I just know."

"But you're pretty happy just with your dad, right?" I began working on a braid on the other side of her head.

"I am. He's the best dad. And if my mom doesn't come back, you could always take her place."

My cheeks heated. "You know your dad and I are just friends, right?"

"Dad says that's how all the best relationships start. Just as friends."

I loved that Michael and Chloe could really talk to each other like this—almost like adults. But I couldn't let her believe something that wasn't true.

I put the last rubber band on her braid and smiled into the mirror. "There you go. You look great."

She grinned. "I like it. Thank you, Elliot."

"You're welcome."

We stood and started to the hallway when I saw Michael there.

Had he heard that conversation? My cheeks warmed at the thought.

I had tried to stay neutral in all my responses because I didn't know where Michael stood with anything concerning Chloe's birth mom. I didn't think I had said anything offensive, but the subject just seemed so delicate.

"Chloe, it's past your bedtime," Michael said.

"But Elliot just fixed my hair!"

"And maybe she can do that again for you another time. But for tonight, you have got to get some sleep or you're going to be a very cranky little girl in the morning."

"Dad . . ."

Michael glanced at me. "See? She's already acting like a teenager."

I smiled and slipped out of the way, not wanting to get in the middle of anything. "I should be going."

"Can you wait around for a few minutes?" Michael asked, pausing by Chloe's door.

"Sure."

He probably wanted to talk about the case. It made sense. There were some things that we shouldn't say in front of Chloe. She was too young to hear too many details.

"Goodnight, Elliot!" Chloe threw her arms around me again.

I pulled her into a hug. "It was really fun tonight, Chloe. Thank you for inviting me."

"Can we do it again sometime?"

"I would like that."

She beamed. "Me too."

And with that, I slipped out into the hallway to give Michael and Chloe a moment together.

CHAPTER TWENTY-SIX

AS MICHAEL TUCKED CHLOE IN, I wandered around his living room. I paused by two bookshelves that guarded either side of the fireplace.

Numerous pictures of Michael in his baseball uniform stood there, as well as a few framed articles detailing his accomplishments and several trophies.

He really had been a big deal, hadn't he? To talk to him now, you wouldn't know that. He seemed so humble and down to earth.

The more I learned about Michael, the more curious I became.

"My mom decorated this for me."

I turned when I heard Michael's voice. He stood behind me. Only a few inches away, for that matter.

"Sounds like something a mother would do. Always ready to brag on her kids."

"My parents are very proud of me." He stared at the photos. "They thought I was going to be in that sport for life."

I turned and leaned my hip against a nearby chair. "What happened?"

"I injured my knee. I couldn't run anymore."

"Were you devastated?"

He shrugged. "I don't know. I'd worked my whole life to get to that point. Maybe it sounds weird since I was only in my early twenties when it happened. But I started playing Little League on those very same fields where we're practicing on right now. Little League turned into year-round baseball. That turned into travel ball, which eventually turned into playing for my high school and later into talking to recruiters."

"And then you did it. You made it to the major leagues."

He rubbed a hand across his chin. "I did. But sometimes you gotta be careful what you wish for."

"What do you mean?"

"I mean, I thought it was what I always wanted to do. But when I got to the top, I found it was more lonely than I ever anticipated. And I found that sticking to my convictions was much harder than I thought. I made a lot of mistakes, mistakes that I can never undo."

I wondered if Chloe's mom was included in those mistakes.

"Well, it seems like you're doing well for yourself now. You're not playing Major League Baseball, but you're helping people who need help, and you have a beautiful little girl who thinks the world of you."

Something shifted in his gaze as he looked at me. "You're right. I can't complain."

I stared at him a moment until I realized that I was staring at him. And then I looked away. But something in his gaze had seemed mesmerizing.

Which was weird. Because Michael was just my friend. I should *not* be staring at him like that.

Suddenly, I straightened. My throat burned as I realized that my emotions and thoughts were going places that I didn't want them to go.

"I should head home," I insisted. "Thanks for everything tonight."

The sooner I got out of here, the better.

I started to breeze past Michael when he grabbed my hand.

I froze. What was happening right now?

As I turned toward Michael, searching his gaze for answers, I felt him pull me close. I felt his arm go to my waist. I felt myself standing entirely too near to him.

And liking it.

Before I realized what was happening, his hands went to either side of my face.

As my gaze fluttered up to his, his lips covered mine. Gently. Firmly.

Until I didn't hesitate.

Then the kiss deepened into something passionate, something that made me forget all my problems.

Lava flowed through my veins while fireworks went off in my head.

It sounded ridiculous, but it was true.

When Michael finally released me, I staggered back, feeling off-balance—in a good way.

No, a confusing way.

No, a good way.

I couldn't make up my mind.

I stared at him, my lips still burning.

"What was that?" My voice nearly sounded hoarse as I choked out the question.

Michael grinned. "That was me kissing you and not apologizing for it."

I let out a quick, airy laugh. He just had to bring that up, didn't he?

But his words reminded me of Hunter. The two of us weren't dating. We were getting to know each other. But . . .

"Michael . . ." I started, unsure what to say.

He took my hand and pulled me closer again, so we were face-to-face. And the way he looked at me right now . . . it wasn't like a friend looked at another friend. There was something deep and warm and smoldering in his eyes. And I felt like I could look at him all day when he had that look in his eyes.

At once, I felt safe, protected, and loved.

All those things made me feel like my head was spinning.

And part of me didn't want it to stop.

"I've been trying to tell myself for weeks now that I was okay with us just being friends," Michael said. "But . . . the more I get to know you, the more I realize that I have never felt the way I feel about you with anybody else."

My heart started pounding in my ears. "Michael . . ."

He pushed a stray hair from my eyes. "You keep saying that. And I'm not sure what it means."

"This is . . ." What was it? And what did I even tell him? "This is surprising."

"Surprising good or surprising bad?" He squinted as he waited for my answer.

I remembered the heat that had run through my veins. It had definitely felt good. Too good.

As I stared up at his face, all I wanted to do was to kiss him again.

He must have seen it in my gaze. Or maybe I initiated it.

But our lips met again. His hand pressed into my back, causing warmth to spread across my skin. His lips tugged mine. Explored mine. Were filled with tenderness yet urgency.

When we pulled away, I nearly felt myself clinging to his chest.

Which was ridiculous.

Kisses like that only happened in the movies and books. Not in real life. And not to me.

Even with Sergio . . . he had never kissed me like that.

Then I remembered Jono's words. His revelation that Michael had stolen a girlfriend from him. Before I let my emotions get too out of control, Michael and I probably needed to talk.

But I also knew it was getting late. Maybe I should put some space between myself and his kiss first.

"I should probably . . . go." My words sounded unconvincing, even to me. That wasn't a good sign.

"I should drive you home," Michael said.

"But you can't leave Chloe."

He frowned. "I should have thought about this earlier. I can wake her up, and she can sleep in the back of the car."

"Don't be ridiculous. I'll be fine." The last thing I wanted to do was wake up Chloe.

He touched my arm, sending another pulse of electricity through me. "Did you forget about that rose with the nautical knot? You driving home by yourself at this time of night is a terrible idea."

I couldn't argue with him. But there had to be some kind of solution. "What am I supposed to do? Call for an Uber?"

"Why don't you stay here?" Michael raised his hands and took a step back. "I'm in no way asking that to be suggestive. You can take my room, and I'll sleep out here on the couch."

I nibbled on my bottom lip. "I'm not sure my mom would approve of that."

He rubbed my arm. "I don't want you driving home by yourself. I really should have thought about it earlier, but I didn't, and I apologize. But even if I stay on the phone with you the whole time as you drive, I still don't feel good about it. It's too risky."

I nibbled on my bottom lip as I considered my options. He had a point. With everything going on, it wasn't a great idea for me to be out alone at this time of night.

"What will people think if they know I stayed here?" I asked.

"For starters, no one's going to know. My parents have plenty of property, and none of the neighbors can see the house. Plus, I don't really care what people think, as long as I know the truth."

He had some valid points. Maybe I was overthinking this. I just wanted to do the right thing—only, sometimes, the right thing wasn't clearly marked on the road signs.

"Okay, I will stay," I finally said. "But I'll take the couch. I'm easy."

Michael gave me a weird look.

"What? Easy as in the opposite of difficult," I explained, wondering why he looked so amused.

A bigger grin spread across his face. "That can have a double meaning here in American culture. I wouldn't say that in a normal dating situation."

I had no idea what he was talking about, but I nodded. "I'm going to call my mom before she gets worried."

Michael nodded. "I'll give you space."

Yes, some space was exactly what I needed right now to clear my head.

CHAPTER TWENTY-SEVEN

"ELLIOT . . ."

I heard the warning in my mom's voice. I'd expected it.

I paced to the corner of the dining room, trying to get far enough away that Michael wouldn't overhear.

"It's not like that," I said. "It's just late, and Michael and I have been working this case."

"And?"

"There have been some suspicious things happening." I tried to skirt around too many details. "It's just not in my best interest to drive back home at this hour."

"I can come pick you up."

"No, no, no. I don't want you out this late by yourself either." The last thing I needed was for her to be a target.

"Elliot Ransom, what have you gotten yourself into?" Even more worry raced through her voice. She knew more than I ever gave her credit for . . . but that didn't stop me from trying to protect her.

"I promise, everything is okay. Michael's daughter is here, and there's nothing funny going on."

"Michael has a daughter?" Surprise laced my mom's voice. My mom had met Michael a couple of weeks ago—by accident.

"That's right. She's seven, and she's a real sweetheart."

She paused for a moment before letting out a long sigh.

"I hope you know what you're doing." Skepticism still stained her tone.

"I do," I assured her. "You just need to trust me."

"Well, I remember what it was like to be young and in love."

I blanched. "In love? Mama, nobody ever said anything about being in love."

"I saw the two of you together. Are you telling me there's nothing there?"

Heat rose up my neck again as I contemplated how to answer. I really didn't want to get into all of these details with my mom, especially since I was still processing all of this myself.

"We're . . . friends."

It was the truth. Sure, Michael and I had just kissed. And it was a great kiss. More than a great kiss. But we hadn't established any type of real relationship yet. And maybe we wouldn't. Maybe we would. It was too soon to really know.

I had so many thoughts I needed to sort out.

"Okay, Elliot. I'm going to trust you. Thank you for letting me know."

"I'll come back to the house first thing in the morning," I told her. "And Mama? Thank you."

Even though I was twenty-seven, my mama didn't want me to grow up. She liked keeping me under her thumb, and there were definitely challenges to still living at home. But I knew she needed me, and that was why I stayed.

As I ended the call, I wandered back into the living room.

I sucked in a breath when I saw Michael sitting on the couch.

He was handsome. I'd always known he was handsome in this slouchy, boyish kind of way. But I hadn't realized just how attracted to him that I was until just now.

I swallowed hard. "Can we talk?"

"I would love to."

I SAT down beside Michael on the couch. As I did, his arm was snaked around the back of the furniture. I wasn't sure what was happening, but I felt myself leaning in toward him. I felt the need—the desire—to touch him. To be closer.

He seemed to feel it too, and his arm slipped around my shoulder.

But I really needed to turn off my emotions right now

and try to use some logic. Whatever the outcome of this conversation, it was a big one. Either Michael and I would remain friends—although, it could be an awkward friendship. Or we would move forward.

Either way, the change seemed big. Maybe even overwhelming.

"We should talk," I said.

Michael shifted ever so slightly. "Of course. What do you want to talk about?"

When he said it like that, with his voice so low and teasing, it made me not want to talk at all.

I pulled in a deep breath and held my ground. "I know we don't talk a lot about your past."

"It's not my favorite subject. But you can ask me whatever you want. I'll answer it." His voice didn't contain any edginess —just sincerity.

I swallowed hard and licked my lips. "Michael, when I was at that golf tournament with Jono . . ."

"Go ahead."

I really hated to bring this up, to ruin the moment. But I needed to know what Michael had to say about Jono's statement.

"Jono told me that you two used to be best friends until . . . you stole his girlfriend."

Michael straightened, his face darkening. "He said that?"

I nodded.

"That's not how it went down." Michael removed his arm

from around me and shifted again so we could look each other in the eye. "We were best friends. That was the truth. We were an unlikely pair, but we were inseparable and did everything together."

"What happened?"

"It was the opposite. I'd just left for college, and my girl-friend stayed here in Storm River. I came home early one weekend to surprise her only to find her in Jono's arms."

"Ouch."

"Ouch is right. I'd never felt so betrayed before."

"What happened next?" I needed to know.

"They both tried to explain that their relationship had just happened. That it wasn't a big deal. But it was a big deal to me. I broke it off with my girlfriend, and Jono and I are no longer friends. You don't do that to friends."

"So why would Jono tell me that you stole his girlfriend?"

"Because Jono always likes to spin things so he comes out on top. It's just the way he is. He probably felt intimi-dated by my relationship with you and wanted to paint me in a bad light. Everything is always a competition with him."

I tried to think through everything that both Michael and Jono had told me. Whose word did I trust more—Jono's or Michael's? That was easy.

Michael's.

Plus, other details fell into place.

"I guess that's how you knew that Jono likes to take his

dates back to his yacht?" I finally said, putting that realization together.

"He's a player. My girlfriend—Krista was her name—she didn't even mean anything to him. They didn't keep seeing each other. I think Jono was just upset because I was headed for the major leagues and he wasn't."

"Where is Krista now?"

"I haven't spoken to her in years. But, last I heard, she moved up in DC."

"I see."

"What else? Do you have more questions for me?"

"You and Oscar," I said. "I don't understand the relationship between the two of you. How in the world did you guys even meet?"

"You're hitting me with all the hard questions right now, aren't you?" Michael offered a fleeting smile.

I wasn't going to apologize. Before I made any kind of choice about my future, I needed the answers.

Michael let out a long breath. "So, Oscar is a long story. I guess I'll go back to the whole Jono and Krista situation."

"Okay . . ."

"I was pretty torn up about what happened. I was a pastor's kid. I'd always lived my life in a fishbowl. Sometimes, it felt more like a shark tank, however. It's hard enough when your parents are in ministry, but when they are practically celebrities around here, that makes it all even harder. They were always on me about what an example I was setting and how I was making the family look. And, for years, I tried hard to make sure I made them proud."

"I'm sure that was a lot of pressure."

"It was. Then I went on to play for the Major Leagues. I met people who weren't following any of the rules that I had been following, yet they seemed so happy. I began to wonder if I had been living my life for a God who didn't really exist. I mean, did I really believe? Or was I just trying to carry on with the way I'd been raised?"

"I think we all get to the point in our faith where we ask ourselves these questions. And they are important questions." I'd reached a similar point in my life.

"I agree. But I decided that if these guys could be happy without God, then so could I."

"What happened next?" I sensed a pivotal part of the story coming up.

"I began living the partying lifestyle. I did everything I was raised not to do. And I do mean almost everything— short of murder and stealing. It was around that time that I met Chloe's mom. I'm not proud of this, Elliot. I'm not proud of it at all." His voice cracked as he stared at the floor and let out a long breath.

I held my breath, sensing that whatever Michael was about to say was hard for him. The way his eyes became hooded and the way his shoulders slumped told me that.

"I met Chloe's mom at a party. We seemed to hit it off. Or at least, we had fun together. We ended up dating for about six months and then she broke up with me. Then she disappeared from my life—until four months later."

My heart pounded in my ears. "What do you mean?"

"One day, she showed up at my doorstep with baby Chloe in her arms. I'd had no idea that she was pregnant."

"Wow." I didn't know what else to say. I couldn't even imagine. "What happened next?"

"I knew I had to make things right. So I decided to take responsibility. I got custody of Chloe three days a week in addition to paying child support. But then one day, when Chloe was just three months old, Roxy—her mom—never came back."

"What happened to her?"

"I don't know." Michael shook his head. "There were no signs of foul play or that anything had happened to her. It was like Roxy just got tired of being a mom and left."

"And that was it? It's just been you and Chloe ever since then?"

"Well, that's where Oscar comes into play," Michael said. "I hired him to make sure that Chloe was really my daughter. When you're in the limelight as an MLB player, you can never be too careful."

"And?"

"She is mine."

I released my breath. "That's good."

"Then I hired Oscar to find Roxy."

"Was he able to?"

Michael shook his head. "No, he wasn't. It's like she disappeared off the face of the earth. I haven't heard from her since that day, as a matter of fact. In return for Oscar's keeping this on the down-low for me, I recommended his services to some of my friends in baseball."

"The whole I'll scratch your back if you scratch mine."

Michael nodded. "When I needed a job, Oscar offered me one. I have been working for him ever since then."

"Wow."

Michael nodded. "Yeah, I know. It's a lot to let sink in. And, Elliot, I never talk about this with anybody. The last thing I want is to have Chloe all over the news featured as some type of scandal."

"I would never want that either," I told him. "Certainly, you know that I'm not the go to the media type of person."

"I know. And I appreciate that about you. But I haven't really dated much since then. My whole life revolves around Chloe. The good that came out of all of this is that I came back home and reconnected with my family. I realized that my faith really could be my own, and I got my life straight again. So maybe I lost everything, but, in doing so, I also gained everything."

I reached forward and squeezed his hand. "I'm glad that the prodigal son returned home."

A slight smile feathered across his lips. "Me too. I don't want to pressure you, Elliot. I know you have a lot on your plate right now too. So you can have all the space that you need."

Relief filled me. I'd never been so glad to hear those words. Because I still had a lot that I needed to work out.

I had to figure out Hunter.

I needed to know that I was truly over Sergio and the heartbreak he had caused in my life.

And then perhaps one of the biggest: Could I really date a coworker? Last time I had done that it had been a disaster.

Instead of thinking about it too much right now, I rested my head on Michael's shoulder.

Maybe in the quiet, I could find some answers.

CHAPTER TWENTY-EIGHT

I WOKE up with a surge of panic the next morning. I was on the couch, and Michael must have tucked a blanket around me.

But what if Chloe saw me here?

Even though I'd stayed over the night before when Michael was sick, something about this felt different. It made me uncomfortable.

I sprang up and quickly found some paper in a kitchen drawer. I left a note for Michael, telling him I would see him at work, and then I slipped outside.

I needed to get home.

As soon as I stepped out the door I glanced around. The hair on my arms rose again.

Was someone watching me? My father's murderer? The Beltway Killer? Coach Cruz's killer?

There were so many options.

I didn't see anyone or anything.

Quickly, I climbed into my car and locked the doors. And then I tried to start it.

Tried being the key word.

The engine wouldn't turn over.

My head fell against the seat for a moment as exasperation enveloped me. Why now?

I gave it one more try, but it still didn't work.

Before I could figure out a Plan B, the front door opened and Michael stepped out. He wore gray pajama bottoms and a white T-shirt and had a sleepy look in his eyes.

I had to admit that it was kind of a good look.

I frowned and reluctantly climbed from the car and met him near the front door.

"You trying to sneak out on me?" He almost sounded amused.

"I just didn't know what Chloe would think." I nodded with my head toward my car. "I guess it doesn't matter, though. Because I'm not going anywhere right now."

"Car problems?"

I nodded.

Just then, Chloe darted out the door and gave my legs a hug again. "Elliot, Elliot, Elliot! You're still here."

I glanced at Michael. "I'm having some car trouble."

"My dad can give you a ride." She looked back at her dad. "Right?"

"Of course, sweetie." He affectionately rubbed the top of her head. "Why don't you run inside and get dressed for school? I'll be right there."

As soon as she disappeared, Michael and I turned to each other.

"How are you this morning?" Something about Michael's voice sounded more intimate than usual.

The sound caused my cheeks to flush again.

I nodded, even though my thoughts were shooting all over the place. "I'm good."

"Are you freaked out?"

I wanted to deny it, but I couldn't. "Maybe a little. I'm a slow processor. I like to take my time with these things."

"And it's fine. Like I said, I'm not going to pressure you. That's a true fact."

I felt so grateful that he was so understanding. "Thank you."

"Listen, I need to take Chloe to school then I'll give you a ride back to your house. I'm sure you're anxious to get cleaned up. And then we can head into work. Sound good?"

I nodded. "That sounds great. Thank you."

But I had to wonder just what today was going to hold.

MY MOM WAS WAITING for me with wide, judging eyes when I walked into my house.

Michael said he was going to run and grab some coffee, but he'd be back in thirty minutes. I assured him that would be just enough time.

Then again, I hadn't factored in my mom's interrogation.

"You look tired." My mom stood in the entryway and scrutinized me.

"That's because I didn't sleep well on the couch," I said as I tried to dodge around her and head toward my room.

"On the couch, huh?"

I paused and turned to her, feeling more exhausted than I would like. "You said you trusted me."

"I do, but . . ."

"But what?" I waited.

She frowned. "I just worry about you, Elliot."

"You raised me up the way you thought you should. Now you need to trust that all your hard work is going to pay off. I was a good girl. I promise."

"I just don't want to see you make mistakes—mistakes that will have an emotional aftermath that you're not going to want to deal with."

"Mama . . ." I tried to keep the exasperation out of my voice. "I appreciate your concern. But you're reading entirely more into this than you should."

She stared at me another moment before nodding. "Okay then. I'm sorry. But I'm a mom, and I'm never going to stop worrying."

I reached forward and kissed her cheek. "And I appreciate that. I just need a little more space sometimes."

She nodded, but I saw the moisture glistening in her eyes. "Get ready. I know you have to go into work today. I didn't see your car out front, though."

I told her what had happened.

Her frown deepened. "More money going into that clunker."

"It's my transportation to and from work," I told her. "I know we're trying to save every dime that we can but . . . I'm going to see if Michael can take a look at it. Maybe he can fix it for me. Now, I really do need to take that shower."

"And I'm going to head to work." She glanced at her watch. "We'll catch up later."

As soon as I was in the shower by myself, I let out a sigh of relief.

While I appreciated my mom, she could be both overprotective and overbearing at times. Times like this I almost wished I lived by myself. I kept telling myself I'd have plenty of time for that later. The rest of my life.

But that area was a gray one. It wasn't all black or all white. The truth was somewhere in between.

Like many things in my life right now.

Finally, I got dressed—keeping in mind I had a funeral later—and hurried back outside to begin my day.

But I knew my troubles were far from being over.

CHAPTER TWENTY-NINE

"YOU LOOK NICE," Michael said as I climbed into his minivan.

I'd put on a black knit dress that came to my knees. "Thank you."

"We have a slight change of plans," Michael told me as he waited for me to pull on my seatbelt. "But, first, I picked this up for you."

He handed me a cup of coffee. It was just what I needed. And if only I had some fresh fruit, my day might be complete.

"Thank you."

"And this." Michael handed me something else.

My eyes widened when I saw a plastic cup full of cantaloupe and grapes. "My hero."

He flashed a smile, but it was fleeting. "Unfortunately, we're not going to have much time."

Something changed in his voice—something bad. "What's going on?"

"The police found Grayson. Somebody left him on the side of the road." Regret stretched through his voice.

My lungs froze, and my heart pounded in my ears. As he said that, I didn't want to say the word floating in my head. The word *dead*.

"He's okay. Beat up, but okay."

I released the breath from my lungs. "That's good news, at least."

"It is. They actually found him last night. The police and the CIA have already talked to him. Grayson called me and told me we could go to the hospital to chat as well. He's been cleared."

"Okay." I hardly wanted to ask the question that was on the tip of my tongue. That question being . . . did Grayson still have the jump drive?

There were far more important things to think about right now. Like the fact that Grayson was okay. That had to be my first priority. But that didn't stop the other questions from pounding in my head.

Whatever was on that jump drive could help me find my father's killer. I couldn't easily dismiss it as unimportant.

Instead, I took a sip of my coffee as Michael headed down the road.

"Did you tell Oscar?" I asked.

"I told him that you and I had some things that we were investigating."

"And if he finds out I'm investigating Grayson, am I going to get fired again?" It was explicitly in my contract that I could not take on any cases outside the ones I was given at the office.

"I think we'll be okay."

I glanced at Michael as he drove. There was so much I wanted to say to him. But I still wasn't sure, out of all the things that wanted to leave my lips, which ones I wanted to hang my convictions on.

I wasn't about to tell Michael how much he meant to me if I didn't think that our relationship was going to work. Nor did I want to tell him that we weren't going to work, only to wake up the next day and regret it.

I took decisions like this probably a little too seriously sometimes.

But as I studied his profile now, I realized how much I did care about him. Did I want to take our relationship to the next level? I still wasn't sure. I could learn to live with kisses like his for the rest of my life, that was certain.

If only relationships just boiled down to sweet kisses.

A few minutes later, we hit the interstate. In less than thirty minutes, we should be at the hospital.

I braced myself for whatever Grayson was going to tell us.

I FLINCHED when I saw Grayson in the hospital bed. I probably wouldn't have recognized him if I hadn't known beforehand who he was. His face was swollen, his eyes were black-and-blue, and his lip busted.

That was only what I could see with my eyes. Who knew what other kind of injuries he had both internally and emotionally?

I remained beside Michael as we approached his bed.

"You look . . ." Michael started.

"Terrible," Grayson said, his voice raspy. "You don't have to beat around the bush."

"I was going to say like you should be on a magazine cover," Michael said.

"Maybe for *Fight Weekly*?"

I was glad to see that both of them still had their sense of humor.

"I'm so glad you're okay," I said. My voice cracked as I said the words.

I had so much emotion inside me. Relief that he had been found. Guilt that he had been taken in the first place. Curiosity over what had transpired in the meantime.

"Me too." All joking disappeared from Grayson's gaze.

"What happened?" Michael's voice turned serious as we waited for his answer.

"One minute, I got out of the shower. The next minute,

two men barged into my apartment. They turned everything upside down until they found the jump drive. I'd hidden it." He frowned as he glanced at me. "I'm sorry, Elliot. I tried to hide it, but it was no use."

"Don't apologize. Please. If anyone should feel guilty, it's me."

"I thought they were going to take the device and leave. But, instead, they took me with them. They tried to get me to access the information on the drive. But I couldn't . . . I needed input from Elliot. That's why I wanted you guys to come by."

"You needed more information from her?" Michael asked.

"That's right. I finally got past the first layer of security, but there was other personal information I needed. It was a multi-layered process. I didn't want to ask you over the phone because I was afraid that somebody was listening in to my calls. Apparently, I was right."

"Did that just start after we dropped off the jump drive?" Michael shifted and crossed his arms.

"That's my best guess." Grayson took a sip of water before continuing. "Maybe somebody was watching you, Elliot, and saw you bring it to me. It's the only thing that I can figure."

Watching me? Yes, they were. I had no doubt about that. "Did you recognize any of those guys?"

He shook his head. "No, I'm sorry. I gave a description of the men to the FBI. Maybe they can figure something out."

"Let's hope," I said. "Were these men able to access it?"

"I don't think so. But they had some guy they were going to take it to who might be able to get into it. If I couldn't do it without information from you, Elliot, then I doubt they can either."

I supposed that was good news. But the bad news was that the jump drive was gone. I wouldn't ever be able to find out what was on it.

I fought a frown.

"Did they leave you on the side of the road?" Michael asked, his eyes narrow as if he tried to put the pieces together.

"No," Grayson said. "They left to meet with someone. When they did, I managed to get my hands and legs free. I got out of the apartment and ran as fast as I could. I finally passed out in the ditch, and that's where I was found."

My hopes lifted. "Are the police checking out that apartment?"

Maybe they could discover something about those men there. Maybe the police would be able to track them down.

"I gave them the description," Grayson said. "They're supposed to be on their way there now."

"Two men abducted you, right?" Michael clarified.

Grayson shook his head. "No, man. There were three."

I frowned as I replayed all the information I'd learned up until today. "Only two were on that video."

"I don't know what to tell you. There were three. The

leader of the pack, a meaty sidekick, and a redhead who talked too much."

The air left my lungs. "A redhead?"

"Yeah, why?"

"Did he have a slight lisp?" I asked.

Grayson nodded. "He did. How did you know that?"

Michael and I looked at each other.

"Because that man was pretending to be your neighbor," Michael muttered. "He was there the whole time, and we didn't realize it."

I let that thought settle for a minute. It definitely wasn't comforting.

We could have had answers by now if we'd realized that earlier.

But we hadn't. And there was no changing that.

"I'm glad you got away when you did," I finally said.

Grayson's gaze met mine, something heavy there. "Elliot, they were talking in Spanish. My Spanish isn't the best. But what they said made my blood cold."

I sucked in a breath. "What was it?"

"That no one was going to stop their plan. They would kill to keep things quiet. And then they said your name."

CHAPTER THIRTY

THE FUNERAL WASN'T for three more hours, so Michael and I stopped by The Board Room so we could discuss things. I figured there was nothing else to discuss concerning Grayson. I knew that the police and the FBI would be looking into that. I had to wonder who had their hands on that jump drive now, though.

But for the moment, I needed to put that aside so I could concentrate on James Cruz's upcoming funeral.

Michael ordered a brunch charcuterie board that came with waffles, fruit, donuts, and bacon. It was just the brain fuel we needed to dive into this. I wished we were just talking, but there was too much going on to make this a leisurely breakfast.

Michael understood that too.

"I think we should review the suspects we have so far," Michael started.

I picked up a waffle, dipped it into some peanut butter syrup, and nodded. "Good idea. My guess is that most of the suspects we have are going to be at this funeral."

"I suspect the same." Michael grabbed a piece of bacon. "Okay, the first person we looked at was Rex Stephens. He was out of town when the accident happened."

"That doesn't mean he couldn't have done something to tamper with the car before he left."

"But we have no evidence that says the car was even tampered with."

"True fact, to use your own phrase."

"I'm teaching you well." Michael grinned. "The next person we looked into was Coach Beasley. His motive isn't the greatest, and he did admit that he sabotaged some equipment. But that doesn't make him a murderer."

"I agree. And it's like you said, he couldn't tamper with the car even if he wanted to since he doesn't know a spark plug from a gas cap."

Michael picked up a waffle but didn't take a bite. "And that brings us to Mischa Harrington. Apparently, she was in love with James. Love and scorned love always seem to be a good motive for murder."

"I don't see her as the type to do something like this, though," I said. "If he was murdered in that supposed car accident, it seems more likely that a man did that. Not to stereotype. But women do have certain methods of murder that are different from a man's, in general."

"I agree. So where does that leave us?"

"Maybe it's somebody we haven't even looked into. There are other people on the team. And we haven't even looked into the Baby Kissers. Or maybe it was Cruz's ex-wife. Or maybe it was Tonya Birdsong. There are so many options here."

"Or maybe it wasn't murder at all."

I tapped my finger against the table. "Okay, let's not look at the suspects, but let's look at the clues. We know that James Cruz seemed distracted over the past couple of weeks. We also know that he had told somebody that he had a good opportunity presented to him."

Michael nodded. "That's correct. However, no one seems to know exactly what that opportunity was. We also know that he was texting somebody right before the accident, which many people have said he would never do."

"But the number was unknown," I reminded him. "And there's a good chance that someone hijacked his phone."

"But we have no idea who."

"And he borrowed money from Mr. Harrington to help someone." I shook my head. "I don't feel like we're getting anywhere with this." In fact, it was making my head pound. I just wanted something to make sense. I wanted an obvious suspect, an obvious motive, and an obvious murder.

Too bad things don't always work out like that, though.

"So what are we going to do?" I asked.

"I say we go to the funeral. You can use your keen powers of observation to watch people's body language. That might tell us everything we need to know."

I frowned, feeling an unusual amount of pressure. "Okay. I hope I don't let you down."

"You could never let me down, Elliot."

I felt myself glow a little at his words. But I still didn't want to let him down.

AS WE CLIMBED into Michael's minivan to drive to the funeral, my phone rang. When I saw the name on the screen, I felt my throat tighten.

I clicked the button to turn down the volume and lowered my phone.

"Is it Hunter?" Michael asked.

I nodded, suddenly feeling very uncomfortable.

"You can answer it, Elliot."

That was just so strange to answer this phone call in front of Michael and in such a small space at that.

But I really wanted to know what he might have to say. For that reason, I hit the button and put the phone to my ear.

"Hey, Hunter," I started. "What's going on?"

So many thoughts collided inside me. It was nice to talk to him. There was nothing about Hunter not to like.

Although he *had* kissed me and apologized for it.

Then again, he had a traumatic romantic past. Maybe that meant he wasn't ready for a relationship.

"I just wanted to call and check on you, especially in light of everything that's going on," Hunter said.

"In light of everything that's going on?" Did he know about Michael and me?

He didn't say anything for a moment. "With the Beltway Killer . . ."

My lungs loosened. Of course. What else would he be talking about? I mentally chided myself.

"No signs of trouble," I said.

Michael started down the road. We didn't have any time to waste if we wanted to get to the funeral in time.

"Good. And I'm sorry about that confusion with the text yesterday. I'm not sure what's going on."

"Anybody would be confused in your shoes. It looks like somehow my phone was hacked."

He paused for a beat. "It does. Doesn't make much sense, does it? That somebody would go through all that trouble just to mess with your head—and mine."

"There's a lot in my life that doesn't make sense right now," I muttered.

"We'll have to talk more about it later. In the meantime, I'll see you at the funeral, okay?"

"I'll see you then."

The funeral itself was going to take place at the baseball

field. Coach Cruz's brother had planned it, and he said this was the way that James would have wanted it. It seemed strange to me, but I held no judgment. Where a person held a funeral was not my business, and I had far greater worries in my life.

A red light flashed in front of us, but Michael didn't slow.

I touched his arm. "You see that, right?"

His brow furrowed. "I do. But . . ."

Something was wrong, I realized.

"I can't stop, Elliot. In fact, my van's accelerating, and I can't do anything about it."

CHAPTER THIRTY-ONE

"WHAT DO you mean it's accelerating and you can't do anything?" I gripped the armrest beside me and tried to calm my racing heart. It didn't work. In fact, it probably raced faster.

He hit the brake and the accelerator, but nothing changed. "It's like something has taken over my van."

I didn't even know how that was possible. All I could think about was how we were going to survive this situation.

I held my breath as we approached the red light.

Michael tugged on the emergency brake, sweat across his brow.

The minivan didn't slow.

I closed my eyes, unable to look. Instead, I imagined the crunching of metal. The squeal of brakes. The feel of death being imminent.

Miraculously, we made it through with just some honks.

"What are we going to do, Michael?" I asked.

"I wish I knew." His jaw tightened. "I've trained for a lot of things, but not this."

"Can you control the steering wheel?"

He turned it, but the van continued going straight toward traffic. "No, I can't."

"Can you pull the key from the ignition?"

He tried. "No, not while the van is in Drive. And it won't let me turn it off."

This was going to end horribly. Of all the ways I had seen myself dying, this was not one of them. And that was saying a lot because I'd even imagined being stampeded by guanacos.

"I hate to say this, Elliot. But we may have to abandon ship."

"But we're not in a ship." What was he talking about?

"I mean, we may have to jump out of this van before it hits something. We don't have another choice."

"But . . ."

"We're going to be bumped and bruised, but it's going to be better than being dead. At least there aren't that many cars on the road right now." He quickly glanced at me, worry saturating his gaze.

He wasn't being flippant. He meant every word he said.

That was true. I could count my blessings in that regard.

The van continued to speed along the road. I knew that we didn't have much time.

"You can do this." Michael stole another glance at me, not bothering to hide his concern. "I know you can. When you land, try to land on your side and roll. Okay?"

I nodded, even though I wasn't sure about anything.

I released my seatbelt and reached for my door handle, but when I tugged it, it wouldn't open. "We're locked in here."

His jaw hardened even more.

As we headed for another intersection, more drivers lay on their horns.

Michael reached into the glove compartment and pulled out some type of device. "Break the windshield."

"What?"

"Tap this against it, and it will break. It's our only choice. The electrical system of this van is completely out of my control."

I raised the device to do just that.

But just as quickly as everything started, the van died.

The vehicle stopped on the road, almost as if nothing had ever happened.

Michael and I sat there for a few minutes, trying to catch our breath.

My heart pounded in my chest as I tried to make sense of what had just happened, but I couldn't.

The only thing I was certain about was that I had a better idea now of how Coach Cruz had died.

And I was certain that it had not been an accident.

MICHAEL PULLED his key from the ignition, breathless as he sat there. "Come on. Let's get out of here before anything else happens."

He didn't have to tell me twice. I tugged on the door handle.

It opened this time.

Wasting no time, I hopped from the van and hurried to the sidewalk. The van was on the side of the street, almost like we'd parked there, even though we hadn't.

Around us, several people had stopped to stare, as if wondering whether we were high or somehow out of our minds.

Michael took my arm. "We need to get to the funeral. This wasn't a coincidence."

"What about the police? Shouldn't we call them?"

"We will—later. Right now, we don't have any time to waste."

My arms were still trembling as we started down the sidewalk. We were only a couple of blocks from the field. We should get there in time.

But my mind raced. The facts were all there in front of me. I just needed to put them together. What was I missing?

"So whoever is behind this was able to send fake text messages to and from the coach's phone," I said. "He was also able to take control of the coach's car and ram it into that tree." In my heels, I struggled to keep up with Michael's quick pace.

"That sounds right," Michael said.

"We also know the coach was in some type of financial trouble. It's the only thing that could explain why he was trying to sell his house and maybe even his car."

"And whoever he was supposed to meet about selling his car may have lured him out in order for that accident to happen," Michael added.

"So he needs money. But how did that lead to someone killing him?"

Michael shook his head. "Maybe he made some type of unscrupulous purchase. Maybe if he went to the authorities, he could have painted somebody else in a bad light."

"It doesn't really rule out many people on the team then. Most of them are wealthy. Almost any of them probably could have let him have the money."

"But now our motives and means are starting to fit," Michael added. "Whoever killed him could do it from the comfort of their keyboard. Maybe even from the comfort of their phone."

I felt certain that this killer was going to be at the funeral. We needed to figure out who he was. Because next time, Michael and I might not be so lucky.

CHAPTER THIRTY-TWO

THE FUNERAL HAD ALREADY STARTED by the time we got there. Coach Cruz's coffin had been placed at home plate, and everyone who'd come to pay their respects had been seated around the diamond. His family—which included his brother, his sister-in-law, and some nieces and nephews—sat in the dugout.

It was unique, but I supposed it fit Coach Cruz.

Michael and I stood at the back of the crowd. Though some seats had been set up, they were all taken. It was just as well. Since I was standing, I had a better view of everybody here.

Mostly, I saw the usual crowd. Almost everybody from the softball team had come. Several people from the other team were also there. Members of what appeared to be the high school baseball team, all wearing their uniforms, stood nearby.

The one thing I knew for sure was that the killer was also most likely here.

"Keep your eyes open for anyone who looks suspicious," Michael whispered.

I nodded. I was already doing that.

As I did, I reviewed all of the facts we'd gone over earlier. This killer was somebody very familiar with technology. And someone who knew quite a bit about money. And someone Cruz had apparently had a falling out with.

I thought I could rule out Mischa. Coach Beasley also seemed to be off my list.

My gaze stopped on Rex. Could he be behind this? The man constantly seemed to be in his father's shadow. But one little fight over his son playing for the baseball team didn't seem enough to justify a murder.

Peter Harrington? I didn't think so.

My gaze stopped on Wally next.

What if he was the one who did this? But why would he have hired us?

Then again, it wasn't beyond the scope of what could happen. People had done crazier things before.

My phone buzzed. I tried not to look at it. I really did. I mean, I knew it was totally uncouth at a funeral to do so.

But it was almost like I couldn't stop myself.

The air left my lungs at what I saw there.

It was a video. Of Michael and I kissing.

I nudged him and turned the screen so he could see. His eyes widened. They widened even more when the video continued and revealed the private conversation we had. The conversation about Chloe's mom.

At the bottom of the video was the text: **Go to the announcer booth now, or I will put this on the screen for everyone to see.**

I glanced at the announcer booth behind home plate. The two-story building had a massive screen on it that was usually used for a scoreboard or to show replays.

I imagined my life playing out there instead of the game.

For Chloe's sake, Michael and I could not let that happen. Some things were meant to be private.

"We have to go," I whispered.

Michael's face looked tense, but he nodded.

I glanced around, looking for a sign of who had sent this. I saw no one suspicious.

Michael and I sneaked around the edge of the field. We reached the announcer booth and grabbed the door. It was unlocked.

Carefully, we slipped inside.

Everything was quiet in here. Quiet and dark.

Michael took my hand and led me up the steps.

My heart thumped out of control as he did.

Michael motioned for me to remain in place while he stepped inside the booth area.

I held my breath as I waited, as I anticipated trouble.

A moment later, he stuck his head out and motioned for me to come inside.

"It's clear," he said. "No one is up here."

I didn't know if I felt disappointed or relieved. Why had someone told us to come up here then?

I glanced at the small desk. At the equipment set up there —none of which I knew how to operate. A small laptop stood in the corner.

Were we missing something right now?

My gaze went out the tinted windows. Most people couldn't see inside here. We could only see them—unless you walked past the area where the window was cracked.

This killer could possibly walk away right now and get away with everything. The police weren't even investigating him.

So why risk everything?

I looked out at the crowd again, scanning them for a sign of anything suspicious.

"I'm not sure why we're here," I said. "But, Michael, the killer thinks we're on to him or her and is getting nervous. It's the only reason your minivan would have been targeted today."

"I agree. The question is why didn't this person just finish us then?"

"Maybe because the funeral started," I realized.

His eyes widened. "The time does match up, doesn't it?"

"It does."

He let out a long breath, and his hands went to his hips. "This has me baffled, I'm not going to lie."

"Whoever is behind this knows a lot about technology." I remembered the phone and the way the minivan had been commandeered.

"Or they hired someone."

My thoughts still churned. "Mischa said her father loaned Cruz some money before he died. He was in debt for some reason. But someone like Cruz . . . he'd need a good reason to risk everything."

"Maybe he gambled on a really good opportunity."

"I did find that receipt from the casino. But I also heard Cruz wasn't a gambler." I chewed on my bottom lip. The answer was right there in front of me.

The killer was someone who knew both technology and money.

I sucked in a breath. There was only one person it could be.

And I'd tell Michael all about it—as soon as we were out of this building.

"Maybe we should go." I suddenly felt too isolated. Even though we were practically in plain view of everybody, I felt like we'd be safer out with the crowd.

Almost as if someone had heard me, the door behind us slammed shut.

Michael yanked on the knob.

It didn't budge.

Had someone locked us in here?

Why would he do that?

And what exactly was he planning?

MICHAEL KICKED THE DOOR.

Nothing.

He gave it another kick.

Nothing.

On the third kick, the wood splintered.

"Let's get out of here," Michael muttered.

Michael grabbed something from the desk before taking my hand. We rushed downstairs, trying to get to safety before this person struck again.

But, as we reached the door leading outside, someone stepped into our path.

Rex Stephens.

Of course.

He was the only one who had made sense. Only I'd realized it too late.

He had a gun in his hands as he stood in front of us, sweat across his brow. "This isn't the way I like to do things."

"Then don't do it." Michael nudged me behind him.

"You guys should have just left it alone. The police

weren't even suspicious. Cruz's death just seemed like an accident."

My heart pounded into my ribcage as I anticipated what might happen next. Certainly, Rex didn't think he was going to get away with shooting us here and leaving us, did he?

I needed to buy time until we could figure out a way to get past him.

"I didn't put the facts together until it was too late," I started. "But everything makes sense now. You talked Coach Cruz into making an investment with your firm, didn't you?"

Rex remained quiet.

"It was a big investment—one that required Cruz to get a loan from Mr. Harrington. There must have been a certain amount needed to buy into this investment. Cruz didn't have quite enough money, but you convinced him the opportunity was too good to pass up."

Rex still said nothing.

So I continued. "But you blundered it somehow. Maybe you swindled the money. Maybe you never invested it at all. Or maybe it was a terrible investment. Whatever happened, Cruz's money was gone."

Rex still said nothing. He just held that gun pointed at us.

In my mind, I could see it all playing out. "Meanwhile, Cruz panicked. He didn't have a rich family to fall back on like you do. He needed that money and tried to convince you to give it to him. He probably felt like you owed him, like you'd stolen it. When you wouldn't give it to him, Cruz got desperate. He followed you—right to that casino. He saw that you were a gambler. But what was he going to do with that information . . . ?"

"He was probably going to blackmail him," Michael said.

"Of course. Cruz thought it was the only way to get results."

"He should have left it alone," Rex finally said, his teeth barely moving. "But he wouldn't."

"Why were you so desperate for Cruz's money?" Michael asked. "If you did everything aboveboard, then you should be in the clear."

The gun trembled in his hands. "I made some bad investments. All I ever wanted was for my father to be proud of me. I couldn't let him find out how much money I'd lost. So I took Cruz's money and used it to replace what I'd lost. I thought it would all work out, that I could use the interest to shuffle things around. No one was going to have to know. But that didn't happen. Nothing paid off the way it should have."

"Cruz was going to sell his house and his car to pay his bills," I said. "He didn't know what else to do since his life savings were gone, and he owed Mr. Harrington money."

"You have to do what you have to do," Rex said. "He insisted to me that he had the money."

"You had to do something to keep Cruz quiet," I continued. "You have a background in computer science. You had the know-how to hijack his phone and to hijack the computer system in his car. Since you were out of town when he died, you were in the clear."

"I decided to have a little fun with your cell phone as well," Rex said. "I thought if I distracted you with some interpersonal drama, maybe you'd have less time to concentrate on this investigation. I saw you and the detective chatting and decided to take a stab at what was going on between you."

"Aren't you clever?" I said through clenched teeth.

"I even hijacked your laptop computer camera." Rex smiled, looking a little too satisfied despite the sickly sweat across his face.

"That's how you captured that video of Elliot and I," Michael muttered.

"I needed something to use as leverage. You two were getting too close to answers." He shoved his gun out farther. "Too close to figuring out that I was the one who killed Cruz."

"Why didn't you just finish us off in the van?" I asked. "You had control of it."

"I was in the middle of it when someone came up to me to talk." Rex scowled. "I had to stop."

"What are you going to do to us now?" I hardly wanted to ask that question. But he stood between us and freedom, and he had a gun in his hands. I had no idea what he was thinking.

"We're going to leave here. And you two are going to take a drive."

I swallowed hard at the thought. It was going to look like we were in a tragic accident, wasn't it? Just like Cruz.

I couldn't let that happen. "If we don't?"

"I'll show that video to everyone." His eyes gleamed with satisfaction. "Everyone will know that you two are an item. That you knocked some woman up, and she left you. That your dad might have been a spy."

I gasped. "How did you know that?"

"I accessed your phone and was able to listen in to some of your conversations. Technology is downright amazing, isn't it?"

I couldn't let that information get out. Not just for my sake, but for my family's.

I felt the stakes rising even more, and panic threatened to rise in me.

I couldn't let it.

Rex raised his gun. I knew he was serious. Rex was going to force us into a car and then make it look like we were in an accident.

I held my breath, unsure how things were going to play out. Unsure of the best move I could make. Unsure if I should even make a move.

"Outside," he ordered. "Now. Before this funeral is over."

As Rex pointed the gun at us, I turned toward him.

I had to stop this.

For Chloe's sake.

I pretended to step toward the door. Instead, I tackled Rex. As my body hit his, the gun blasted.

My heart pounded furiously. Had I been hit? Had Michael?

Everything slowed around me.

Please, don't let Michael be hurt. Please.

I still had some fight left within me.

And so did Rex.

He struggled beneath me.

I glanced to the side.

The gun lay beside his hands.

I lunged toward it, trying to reach it before he could grab it again.

But I was too late.

His fingers grasped it.

Before he could raise it in the air, Michael grabbed a bat. He swung it at the weapon.

Rex yelped and dropped the gun to the floor.

Just then, the door flew open. "Police!"

As officers flooded into the space, someone pulled me off Rex.

I turned around and saw Michael.

In one piece.

I jumped to my feet, threw my arms around him, and pulled him close. I was so glad that he was okay. I couldn't bear the images that had gone through my mind.

"You shouldn't have done that," Michael murmured in my ear.

"I couldn't let him ruin your life," I said.

"But you could have gotten killed in the process."

I held him closer, never wanting to let go.

"Good job, guys," a new voice said.

I looked over and saw Hunter standing there, staring at us with a strange expression in his eyes.

He knew, didn't he? Without me saying anything to him, Hunter was able to tell that there was something between Michael and me.

"How did you know to come?" I asked.

"I heard the gunfire," he said. "I also heard him confess to killing Cruz."

"What?"

Michael held something up. "I pressed the button. Everyone at the funeral heard his confession."

I let out a relieved laugh. "Really?"

Michael grinned. "Really. And that's all they heard."

I released my breath. That was good news. Really good news.

"I'm going to need to ask the two of you some questions," Hunter continued.

"Of course," I said.

I was just glad this was over. It was one more thing I could mark off.

But all my worries were far from being over.

CHAPTER THIRTY-THREE

"HEY, BATTA, BATTA, BATTA!" the other team yelled.

If Mischa got a run, the Bigwigs would win the game. Even I, someone who hated sports, felt supercharged. We were sooo close.

I held my breath as I waited to see what would happen. Everyone had played so well. I was proud of them.

And I was proud of Michael. He glowed as he was out on the field.

"Do you think we're going to win?" Chloe asked.

She was sitting on the bench in the dugout beside me. "I think we are. How about you?"

Before she could answer, Mischa swung.

And missed.

I bit back a groan.

"I think we will," Chloe said.

The pitcher threw the ball again.

Mischa swung and missed.

Again.

"That's okay," I called. "You can do it, Mischa!"

I could see her nerves getting the best of her. She looked tense, and I couldn't blame her.

This game was on her shoulders.

As the pitcher sent the ball flying again, the air in my lungs froze.

A second later, I heard a crack.

The bat and the ball had connected!

Mischa dropped the bat and took off toward first base.

The next minute, Mr. Harrington flew across the home plate.

"We won!" I shouted.

Chloe threw her arms around me.

Michael let out a whoop. A moment later, he crossed into the dugout and gave both Chloe and me a hug.

"You did it," I told him.

"We did it." He winked. "Come on! Let's get out on the field."

A certain sense of pride filled me as we all exchanged high fives and atta boys.

We had a win. I could use some of those in my life, whether while investigating or while on the baseball field.

And now that this was over, I needed a moment alone with Michael. The two of us needed to talk.

CHLOE RAN off to play at the playground for a few minutes. I watched her chasing some other kids and smiled.

Michael appeared beside me a moment later, a hot dog in hand. "For you."

"I'm starving." I took it from him. "Thank you."

"You did a good job out there. It's the least I can do."

I took a bite. "This is good."

"They're always better with baseball."

I ate for a few minutes in silence.

"We found that rose almost six days ago," I finally said. There was no need to dance around the fire anymore.

He shoved his hands down into his pockets. "I know."

"No one has been reported missing." Nausea churned in my stomach as the words left my lips.

"I know."

"Maybe Hunter misread the evidence." We both knew my words weren't true.

"We've got to keep our eyes wide open. Hunter did say that anyone affiliated with the softball team might be a target. Or it could be an associate of someone affiliated with the team."

I wished that made me feel better. It didn't.

I started to take another bite of my hot dog and stopped. I couldn't pretend like everything was normal. It wasn't. There were still more conversations to be had.

I swallowed hard and gathered my thoughts.

I remembered talking to Grayson when we'd first met. He'd told me that Michael was loyal, that once he let a person in his circle they were a friend for life.

I liked that.

And I liked Michael.

"I . . . was totally taken by surprise when you kissed me," I started. "I'm not going to lie."

"Nor would I want you to. True fact."

I fought a smile. "I needed to make sure that I was ready for a relationship, especially after Sergio. And then there was Hunter. Then there was the fact that someone might be trying to kill me."

Michael waited, not saying anything.

"That said, I'm willing to give this thing between us a try if you are."

"Don't force yourself . . ." He tilted his head, almost comically.

I let out a little laugh. "That's not what I mean. I'm sorry. I'm not very good at this."

"It's okay, Elliot."

I reached forward and touched his hand. "I'm trying to say that I really like you, Michael."

He grinned. "You just made me the happiest guy around, Elliot Ransom."

Slowly, he leaned down and brushed his lips against mine.

When we pulled away, I said, "Maybe we shouldn't tell Oscar."

He laughed. "Maybe we shouldn't. Not at first, at least. Let's take it slow."

"What about Chloe?" I pictured the little girl. She'd quickly won a place in my heart.

"Let's give ourselves a little time before we tell her. Once she knows, the pressure will be on."

"What pressure?" I asked.

"The pressure for us to a plan a wedding."

I let out a chuckle. "Yes, we should wait then."

Michael took my hand into his.

And it just felt right. Like it fit. Like we belonged together.

I hadn't even been looking for love, but it looked like I may have found it. Or the beginnings of it, at least.

Just like softball required practice, so did investigating and so did learning how to make a relationship work. You had to just be willing to put in the time. Practice didn't make perfect, but practice did make permanent.

Now I just prayed the Beltway Killer gave me the chance to finish exploring those possibilities.

COMING NEXT: THE SKILL OF SNOOPING

ALSO BY CHRISTY BARRITT:

THE WORST DETECTIVE EVER:

I'm not really a private detective. I just play one on TV.

Joey Darling, better known to the world as Raven Remington, detective extraordinaire, is trying to separate herself from her invincible alter ego. She played the spunky character for five years on the hit TV show *Relentless*, which catapulted her to fame and into the role of Hollywood's sweetheart. When her marriage falls apart, her finances dwindle to nothing, and her father disappears, Joey finds herself on the Outer Banks of North Carolina, trying to piece together her life away from the limelight. But as people continually mistake her for the character she played on TV, she's tasked with solving real life crimes . . . even though she's terrible at it.

USA Today has called Christy Barritt's books "scary, funny, passionate, and quirky."

Christy writes both mystery and romantic suspense novels that are clean with underlying messages of faith. Her books have won the Daphne du Maurier Award for Excellence in Suspense and Mystery, have been twice nominated for the Romantic Times Reviewers' Choice Award, and have finaled for both a Carol Award and Foreword Magazine's Book of the Year.

She is married to her Prince Charming, a man who thinks she's hilarious—but only when she's not trying to be. Christy is a self-proclaimed klutz, an avid music lover who's known for spontaneously bursting into song, and a road trip aficionado.

When she's not working or spending time with her family, she enjoys singing, playing the guitar, and exploring small,

unsuspecting towns where people have no idea how acci-
dent-prone she is.

Find Christy online at:
    www.christybarritt.com
    www.facebook.com/christybarritt
    www.twitter.com/cbarritt

Sign up for Christy's newsletter to get information on all of her latest releases here: **www.christybarritt.com/ newsletter-sign-up/**

If you enjoyed this book, please consider leaving a review.